Praise for

Carol Lynne and T.A. Chase

...a well-conceived and multifaceted novella that combines a somewhat gruesome ghost story, an intriguing mystery and m/m romance...chilling and involving and a good read overall
~ *Bookwenches*

I admit that usually I don't read books that falls into the horror genre...I decided to give it a chance and I'm glad I did...a well plotted and written book, filled with great characters, a vividly described locale and a great background event that pulls the reader into the story and keeps their interest from beginning to end...take my advice and give this horror story a try
~ *Literary Nymphs Reviews*

Total-E-Bound Publishing books by Carol Lynne & T.A. Chase:

Dracul's Revenge
Dracul's Blood
Anarchy in Blood

THE HAUNTING OF ST. XAVIER

CAROL LYNNE
& T.A. CHASE

The Haunting of St Xavier
ISBN # 978-0-85715-417-0
©Copyright Carol Lynne & T.A. Chase 2011
Cover Art by April Martinez ©Copyright 2011
Interior text design by Claire Siemaszkiewicz
Total-E-Bound Publishing

Published in 2011 by Total-E-Bound Publishing, Think Tank, Ruston Way, Lincoln, LN6 7FL, United Kingdom.

Total-E-Bound Publishing is an imprint of Total-E-Ntwined Limited.

Manufactured in the USA.

THE
HAUNTING OF
ST. XAVIER

Dedication

Over a year ago, I told my yahoo group about a bloody nun I'd dreamed of. They continued to poke and encourage until I finally asked T.A. if she would please consider helping me give voice to my nightmare. Thanks to my yahoo group, T.A., and the twisted world my mind travels to nightly – Carol Lynne

I was thrilled when Carol asked me to help her bring the bloody nun to life. Thank you, Carol, and your yahoo group who encourages us every minute – T.A. Chase

Prologue

June 18, 1962

It's late as I'm writing this. The small candle in my room is the only illumination I dare provide myself. I know they're watching me, wondering how I'll handle the day's events. It started as a normal Tuesday but ended in a nightmare I shall never rid myself of. Opening the door to St. Xavier, none of us knew what we would find. Hours of unanswered phone calls had caused enough concern that the Father felt the need to investigate. I was at first proud that I'd been one of two chosen to accompany the Father to the monastery. It seemed my years of training, prayer and hard work would finally be noticed by the church.

None of us expected the carnage we found within the walls of the magnificent stone building. We found the Mother Superior in her office. Her throat was slashed, her eyes removed. That was when we heard the first scream.

We rushed towards the staircase. The higher we went, the more blood we found. Each room we entered appeared washed in blood, bodies mutilated, eyes removed. The screaming continued.

The Father was the first to realise the screams were coming from the fourth floor.

Ashamed as I was, I tried to hold the bile down, but it would not be quelled. I emptied my stomach on the landing to the third floor. Although we didn't investigate the third floor, it was obvious the entire building would be forever damned. One of the nuns had obviously tried to crawl out of her room, her body barely making it past the threshold before it had bled out.

With trepidation the three of us continued towards the screams that were growing weaker and weaker by the minute. The Father told me to stand back as he opened the door to the fourth floor offices.

Once the door was opened and we had ascended the last set of stairs, I heard Father Clennan. I couldn't make out what he said, but his voice was calm, almost placating. I was once again told to stay back as the Father and the other entered the room. I was able to catch glimpses of a woman. Her bloodstained tunic was the only hint that she'd once been one of God's chosen children. The sunlight outside the window made the gilded cross in her hand appear to glow as she swung it wildly at Father Clennan. The vile words spewing from her mouth were in direct contrast to Father Clennan's calm tone.

They've come to check on me. I'll finish the rest once eyes are no longer upon me. I pray the church will be able to overcome the tragedy of this day.

Chapter One

Signing his name with a flourish, Jason fought the surge of happiness threatening to overwhelm him. After six months of negotiations, he finally had his hands on what could be the biggest venture of his life.

"Here are the keys to the doors and to the gate." The real estate agent's tight smile spoke of relief more than happiness over the huge commission she'd just made.

"Thanks. I appreciate all the work you did to help me get this." Jason took the keys and shook the lady's hand.

"Well, you were very determined, and the building's just been standing empty since the sixties." She shrugged. "To be honest, I never thought I'd find a buyer."

"Why?" He turned to study the large stone building standing rather forlornly behind the wrought iron gate. "It's gorgeous and absolutely perfect for what I'm planning."

"The problem isn't how the place looks. I think it has more to do with what it was used for, the tragedy that took place here and all the rumours surrounding it."

Frowning, he shot a glance over at her. "Rumours? About what?"

She waved her hand dismissively. "All the usual ones about it being haunted by the nuns who were murdered. Strange screams being heard when there's no one around. I'm not sure anyone has actually spent any time on the property, except for the man you sent over to appraise it."

Jason doubted any of the reports were true. Abandoned buildings, especially ones with twisted pasts, tended to get a creepy reputation after a while. He didn't believe in spirits or ghosts. Hell, he didn't want to think about hanging around this world after he died.

His real estate agent seemed to shake off her melancholy thoughts. "You never did say what you were going to use the property for."

The woman must not have done her homework. The Bentley Corporation, of which Jason was CEO and founder, was the premier builder of gay resorts, but this venture was all about sex. He planned on creating the world's foremost gay erotic resort.

"I'm going to open a resort. The original building is big enough to offer a bunch of rooms, plus I plan on building smaller, more private bungalows around the grounds. I love the English garden, and I'll bring in landscapers to work on getting it back into shape."

"Oh good." She checked her watch. "Well, I need to be going if I'm to get these forms filed with the county clerk's office in time."

Jason hid his smile. He could get carried away with his visions, and not everyone saw them as clearly as he did.

"Thank you again. I'll keep your office in mind if I'm looking to pick up more land in the area."

He watched her drive away, barely managing to contain his excitement and eagerness to tour the property on his own. He waited until her car disappeared from sight before strolling up to the huge iron gate. He studied it for a second, tracing the scroll work with his gaze. 'St. Xavier' was spelt out in iron as well in the arch over the moving part of the gate. He would keep that, though the rust needed to be removed and the scroll work repainted. He liked the old-fashioned feeling it gave to the grounds.

Inserting the key into the lock, he paused and it was like the entire world froze with him. Almost like every living creature held its breath, hesitating while he thought about opening the lock. The strangest sensation washed over him and his hands trembled. Owning the monastery and stepping onto the grounds at this moment seemed like the most important thing he'd ever done. His life was going to change, Jason could feel that, but he didn't know if it would be a good change or bad.

The sound of a car passing by on the road broke the spell and he laughed at himself. Foolish thoughts. It was just the joy of taking this next step in reaching for that elusive thing called happiness. If he achieved his goal of creating the world's most exclusive gay resort, then maybe he could silence all those voices in his head telling him he wasn't good enough.

The key turned in the lock, and he shoved the gate open. The metal hinges screeched like a woman being attacked. Jason cringed and frowned. The agent had sworn all the locks, hinges, and doors were in working condition, as had the appraiser Jason had hired to look at the property. He'd ask the contractors to take a look at the hinges. He would replace them if it looked like they would be more work than he'd thought.

He considered getting his car and driving up to the imposing structure, but he wanted to soak in the overall ambience of the place. The trees hung over the driveway, creating an oppressive feeling of being trapped as Jason wandered along. Those would have to be cut back. He pulled out his notebook and jotted it down. The driveway itself was in good condition, though the grass seemed to have taken over. Made sense considering there hadn't been many visitors since the monastery closed down suddenly all those years ago.

He stretched, trying hard to ignore the sensation of being watched. There wasn't anyone else on the property. The real estate agent had assured him that not even rebellious teenagers sneaked onto the grounds. Jason found that hard to believe, but maybe the kids didn't do things like that in this town.

He made his way to the sidewalk leading up to the front door and stopped, his gaze going to his newest purchase. It was four floors of hulking hand-cut stone, built back in the 1800s when masonry was a craft and the stonemasons had pride in their work. Large windows peered down at him, creating a feeling of brooding disapproval.

Jason smirked. Maybe the imagined disapproval was because of what he planned to do with the monastery and the fact that the Church would have a coronary when and if they found out. He shrugged and headed to the front door. It didn't matter to him what anyone thought of his dreams or his lifestyle for that matter. He wasn't hurting anyone, and he had fun along the way.

The foyer was grand, with vaulted ceilings and a mosaic tiled floor in a stunning sunburst pattern. A few of the tiles were broken or chipped, but Jason knew a man in California who did wonderful reproduction work. He'd replace the broken ones, yet keep the floor the way it had been.

As he moved from room to room, Jason was amazed by the condition of the interior. Aside from dust and a little rodent damage, everything was in relatively good shape. A few of the windows on the ground floor were broken, so he took care to avoid the glass shards as he took inventory, surprised there wasn't water damage on the solid wood floors.

Soon his notebook was full of reminders and ideas for the different rooms. When he had first expressed interest in St. Xavier, the real estate agent had taken him on a tour of the main building. He was completely sold after the first floor, but had gone as far up as the second. His time was valuable, and he always knew what he liked upon sight. Checking his watch, he realised he had plenty of time before his meeting with the local bank manager to inspect the top floor for damage. Although the roof seemed sound, with a building as old as the monastery there were bound to be small leaks here and there.

Jason climbed the stairs, inspecting each floor and marking where attention would be needed. He arrived at the door to the fourth floor and shrugged. He'd been told the fourth floor had been designed and used for meetings and administrative purposes. Normally he would have had the door removed, but his architect believed it would make the ideal location for Jason's living quarters, which he maintained in all of the hotels he owned, as well as an apartment for the manager he'd yet to hire. Jason turned the knob, but the wooden door didn't budge. Frowning, he wiggled the handle, but nothing happened. The door didn't appear to be locked, just stuck. Had something fallen and blocked the door?

He put his full weight behind his push, still it didn't move, but something like a thud sounded in the room. Pressing his ear to the panel, he strained to hear anything. A faint scratching noise floated to him. He stepped away, folded his arms over his chest, and glared at the barrier blocking him.

Great, he had mice or something living up there. Probably those fucking flying squirrels that shit on everything and destroyed stuff with their teeth. He tugged his notebook out of his back pocket and wrote down a note to get an exterminator in as soon as the door could be opened.

As Jason turned to head back downstairs, an ice cold breeze blew past him. Gooseflesh covered his skin and the hair on the back of his neck stood on end. He shuddered, searching for the source. There wasn't an open or broken window to be seen.

Suddenly Jason wanted to get the hell out of the building. Every instinct screamed at him to leave. He looked back over his shoulder at the door to the fourth floor. It might have been the middle of the day, with the sun illuminating the rest of the house, but in the area around that door it was as dark as tar. He blinked twice but each time, the darkness remained. In fact, it looked like it was growing, moving towards him with implacable determination.

His nerve broke and Jason trotted downstairs, not looking back. He locked the front door behind him before heading into the garden. A stone bench appeared alongside one of the paths, tempting Jason to sit until his legs were strong enough to hold him again. He scrubbed a trembling hand over his mouth, breathing deeply to calm his racing heart.

"What the fuck was that?" he muttered aloud.

The words of the agent played through his mind again. 'There are rumours of the monastery being haunted'. He grunted. He didn't believe in ghosts, spirits, or anything supernatural. The world had plenty of evil people in it without making stupid shit up to scare children.

His gaze skipped over the ragged flower beds. The slowly-invading ivy threatened to overtake most of the paths winding through the garden. He could tell it was a classic English version of a garden. A smile broke over his face. Maybe there would be room to put in a hedge maze. He'd loved the ones he'd visited while touring the United Kingdom several years earlier.

Statues were another thing the garden needed, but not just any Renaissance reproductions. He wanted erotic sculptures of men doing naughty things to each other. The landscaper could tuck them into corners where guests of the resort would happen upon them and maybe get ideas from them. One of Jason's fellow business associates had mentioned knowing an artist who created such things. He'd have to get the person's number.

With his legs strong enough to once again support him, Jason pushed to his feet and meandered through the neglected grounds, noting where smaller buildings were and which ones needed to be fixed or demolished. There were several secluded spots, hidden by trees or bushes, where Jason could envision private cabins or bungalows where guests could indulge themselves in all that the resort would offer.

A blood red rose caught his attention and he bent to smell it. Inhaling its scent, he grinned. Looking at him, no one would ever believe he liked flowers. Being six-five, and over two hundred pounds of pure muscle, he didn't inspire many men to think he'd enjoy romantic gestures like a bouquet of flowers or a candle-lit meal. Yet he liked them as much as any other man. Maybe more because growing up, he'd never seen the softer side of life.

He'd lived as close to the poverty line as a person could get without being called poor. His parents had worked hard, but it had always seemed to be a struggle to keep their heads above water. There was barely enough money for food, and definitely never anything left over for frivolous things like flowers or anything special. That's why Jason had worked as hard as he could to get out of the small West Virginia hill town he'd grown up in.

He rubbed his thumb over the velvety petals of the rose and thought of how much his mother would have loved to get her hands on the garden. He'd inherited his love of beautiful things from her. They might not have had much, but she'd checked art books out of the library and they would spend hours looking at the paintings. They'd discussed the ones that called to them and why they liked them so much.

Sorrow swelled in his chest and he absently pressed the heel of his hand against it. No point in thinking about her now. His mother had died when he was ten, worn out before her time from scraping a living from the hard ground they'd called home. Too much work and not enough play time, though there was a lot of love. Even his father—who had worked the coal mines—had tried his best to make life fun for Jason and his sister. At least until his death when Jason had been barely fifteen.

He dug in his jacket pocket, found his phone and contemplated calling his sister, but Joanie was in some exotic locale, shooting models for a clothing line. He didn't want to bother her just because he was homesick. Instead, he dialled his assistant.

"*The* Bentley Corporation, Roland Harkin speaking."

"So professional of you. I'm proud." Jason chuckled.

"Omigod, Jason. Where have you been? Have you signed the papers yet? Is it a done deal? When can I rally the troops and get them heading out to you?"

Jason closed his eyes and brought up the image of Roland in his mind. His personal assistant was the most amazingly organised man on the planet, but very excitable as well. Roland would be pacing his office, hands waving around while he talked. He had broken three phones by throwing them across the room — by accident of course — before Jason had bought him a headset. It was cheaper in the long run.

"Take a breath, dear." He strolled back to the bench and sat, leaning back on one hand while stretching his legs out in front of him. "I've been checking out my newest purchase. The agent said she'd drop the papers off at the court house when she got back into town. So you should probably call and double check that she's filed them, but wait until tomorrow. There's no rush on it."

"Okay." Roland mumbled under his breath and Jason knew the man was typing that into his laptop. "Now which contractors do you want to use? When do you want them out there?"

"Well, as much as I'd like to use companies that are familiar to me, I think it would be smart to see what's available around here first. I know I'm going to need that tile guy we've used before. Call him up and see if he can send someone out to give us an estimate. Also, remember that sculptor we heard about a couple of months ago?"

Roland hummed softly while he thought. "Oh yes. Mr. Hampton mentioned him."

"See if you can get his number and ask if he would be available for some commissions. I have some great spots in the gardens here that would be perfect for his statues."

"Oooh...I'd love to watch him create those." Roland panted.

"Stop it. I need you to focus on work, not getting laid by some hot artist."

"You're no fun."

Jason could tell Roland was pouting and he laughed.

"That wasn't what the little blond said when I dropped him off at his apartment on my way to the airport this morning."

"God, now you're teasing me."

"I don't tease. I make good on everything I say." He chuckled at Roland's groan.

They flirted with each other, but they knew it wouldn't work between them. Roland was too high-maintenance for Jason. He had too many other things going on in his world to place another man in the centre of it at the moment.

"Fine. Be a meanie and not tell me any juicy details." Roland sniffed once before getting down to business. "I'll do some research and see which local construction company looks the most qualified. Also, I'll get you meetings with those two other men. Tell me, does St. Xavier Monastery look to be the perfect place for gay men to act out their deepest fantasies?"

"It's everything I thought it would be when I first spotted the listing." Jason looked around him. "Once it's fixed up, it'll be the most exclusive resort in the world, and you'll be able to buy that cute little Beemer you were drooling over last week."

"Sweet. I'll start picking out the colour. The numbers and names of the potential people will be in your inbox tomorrow morning. Take care and don't do anything I wouldn't do."

"Honey, that leaves so much stuff for me to do, my mind boggles at the thought."

"Asshole."

"Bitch." He shot back. "I'll check in tomorrow."

"Bye."

Hanging up, he laughed. God, Roland could be a flaming bitch at times, but for the most part, the man kept Jason's chaotic life in order and had become a friend in the process. He put his phone away and stood.

Time to meet with the banker and grab something to eat. He'd been on the go since six that morning after spending the night before fucking some cute twenty-one year old he'd brought home from the club. Stupid idea really, considering how much work he had to do, but hell, he'd needed to work off some energy and going to the gym at two in the morning wasn't an option.

Jason locked the gate behind him and climbed into his rental. He glanced back once more and something moved in one of the windows on the fourth floor. Shaking his head, he made a mental note to find an exterminator as soon as possible. They needed to get rid of whatever was living on the top floor before it caused a problem with his plans.

* * * *

Deacon Ryan Christopher sat silently at Father Paul's side, listening to Rita Dorsel explain her husband Jack's sudden change in personality.

"I just don't understand what's going on, Father. Two days ago he was fine. He went to appraise that old monastery on Peachtree and was a little odd-acting when he came home that night, but it seemed to get worse as the evening went on. By yesterday morning, he was delusional." She worried the tissue in her hand for several moments before dabbing at her nose. "Jack's always been a good man."

"Yes, he has," Father Paul agreed. "Have you consulted a physician?"

Rita shook her head. "I can't get him to go, and quite frankly, I can't stand to be in the same room with him. He's vile." Rita closed her eyes and shook her head. "I'm sorry. I know I shouldn't say that about my husband, but it's true."

Father Paul gave Rita's hand a supportive pat. "Where's Jack now?"

Rita sniffled and pointed towards the backyard. "He's in the garage."

Ryan stood, hoping to be the one sent out to talk to Jack. He was overdue to take his final vows and was still not sure if he was following the path he was meant to take. Perhaps reaching out to a man in need would bring him the peace he couldn't seem to find within himself lately.

"I'd be happy to check on him," Ryan offered.

"Not alone!" Rita shouted, covering her mouth after the outburst. "I mean, Jack isn't himself. If you're planning to go out, please go together. He has a sudden hatred for the Church." Rita leant forward. "I think something happened to him at that monastery."

Ryan regarded Father Paul, who sat silently with his head bowed in obvious prayer. He glanced back at Rita and gave her what he hoped was a reassuring smile. "Would you like us to convince Jack to see a doctor?"

"Of course, but in my heart, I don't think his problems are medical," Rita said.

Ryan shuffled his feet, hoping he wasn't about to step over the line. "You think it's mental?"

Rita slowly shook her head from side to side. "I think it's spiritual. It's like the soul of the man I've lived with for twenty-eight years is gone." She snapped her fingers. "Just like that, poof. He leaves for work and comes home..." Before she could finish her sentence, Rita broke down in tears. "Excuse me," she said, rushing from the room.

"Should I go to her?" Ryan asked, unsure of what to do.

Paul's head finally lifted. "No. Helping Jack is the best thing we can do for Mrs. Dorsel."

Ryan nodded. He helped the older priest to his feet and led the way to the backyard. Ryan clutched in his hand the one thing that gave him daily strength, the Bible his mother had given him, or rather had left behind when she'd run out of his life when he was a boy.

It was a warm day, so Ryan was surprised to find the garage door closed. He glanced over his shoulder at Father Paul and pointed towards the large door. "Does that seem strange to you?"

Paul nodded as he absently fingered the large cross hanging around his neck. "Let me knock on the door. I've known Jack for years."

Ryan stopped and nodded, giving way to Father Paul as they reached the side door of the garage. Although he felt unsettled by the soon-to-be confrontation, his unease turned to fear when he noticed Father's Paul's hand shaking as he knocked.

The man who had been his rock during the previous year was scared, a first as far as Ryan had witnessed. "Father? Are you okay?"

Father Paul turned. "I don't feel right."

Ryan stood in silence as sweat began to drip down Father Paul's brow, his complexion turning a subtle shade of grey. "Shall I call someone?"

Father Paul shook his head. "I need to do this."

Ryan stepped forwards and pounded his fist against the wooden door. "Mr. Dorsel? Sir? It's Deacon Christianson and Father Paul from Holy Assumption. Your wife is worried about you."

"No! Stay away from me," Jack screamed through the door. "It's all your fault. You've done this!"

Sounds of objects being thrown against the door had Ryan taking a step back. "Sir? We just want to help you."

"No you don't. You want to shut me up. I know your kind. I've seen what you do!" Jack screamed again.

"I think we should call the police," Ryan said to Father Paul.

With watery eyes, Father Paul nodded. "I'm afraid you may be right. I'll ask Rita if we can use her phone."

Jack continued to rage while Ryan, disturbed by Jack's statements, watched Father Paul walk back to the house. He'd never been the object of so much hatred. What could have happened to Jack Dorsel?

Ryan heard Jack speaking, but it wasn't loud enough for him to understand. "Are you ready to talk to me?" he asked.

"They're crying!" Jack yelled. "I can't shut them up and there's so much blood."

Ryan jumped at the loud sound of a gun going off. "Jack!"

Chapter Two

The morning of Jack Dorsel's funeral, Ryan sat on his bed in the rectory and tried to make sense of the events that had led up to the older man's death. After he'd heard the shot, his safety had no longer mattered. He'd kicked at the door with all that he had, but his small stature was no match for the strong deadbolt.

He'd given up after several attempts and run to one of the small, covered windows. Using his elbow, Ryan had broken the glass, cutting himself in the process, but he hadn't cared. He'd wriggled his lean frame through the small opening and past the faded yellow curtains to find Jack Dorsel lying in a pool of blood, gasping.

Ryan had ripped off his black suit coat and tried to wrap it around Jack's head. The fear in Jack's eyes as Ryan tried his best to save and comfort him was something Ryan would never forget.

A knock sounded at his door. "May I come in?"

"Yes," Ryan answered.

Father Paul stepped into the room and stood beside the door. "You didn't come down for breakfast, so I thought it best to check on you."

"Thank you, Father, I'm just not hungry."

"How's your arm?" Father Paul asked, gesturing to the loosely covered row of stitches.

"Healing." Ryan gazed down at his clasped hands. "I've been trying to make sense of it all, but I'm not having much luck."

Father Paul walked over and placed a hand on Ryan's bowed head. "Sometimes there is no sense to be made out of our actions. Brother Jack was obviously disturbed."

Ryan looked up into the priest's eyes. "What do you think he meant when he said it was our fault? Just before he shot himself, he said, 'They won't stop crying'. Who do you think he was talking about?"

Father Paul shook his head. "We'll never know. I realise it was disturbing for you, but you'll have to move on."

"How can I?" Ryan asked. "He took his own life. He won't even have the peace of heaven to comfort him."

"You have the ability to lend comfort to his widow and to other members of the congregation."

"Yes, Father."

Father Paul's comforting hand squeezed his shoulder. "Trust in God."

Ryan nodded and watched as Father Paul left the room. *Trust in God.* Ryan sighed. He'd spent the previous six years trusting in his faith even though he'd known his sexual preferences weren't in line with the teachings and beliefs he'd grown up with in the church.

While most gay men worried about coming out to their friends and family, Ryan had always been more concerned with coming out to himself and God. It was a constant battle within his heart, becoming ever worse the closer he came to his ordination.

He sighed and lay back on the bed. It was his own fault he was questioning his decision. Five months earlier, he'd counselled a young man who was trying to deal with his homosexual desires. After spending countless hours with Toby, Ryan had realised they were both struggling with the same issues. Even though he hadn't gone as far as to speak about his own internal demons, he had assured Toby he understood what he was going through.

Everything had come to a head a few months earlier when he'd spotted Toby in the back of the congregation, sitting beside another handsome young man. After the service, Toby had introduced Ryan to his new boyfriend and apologised for not being in attendance the previous weeks. He'd explained to Ryan that he'd found a church where it was okay to worship as well as love whom he chose.

Ryan had wished them both well, and he'd genuinely meant it. He only wished his own problems could be worked out as easily.

Rolling onto his side, Ryan yawned. His sleep had suffered since the shooting. He'd been mere feet from Jack and hadn't been able to stop him. What if he'd tried harder to get the confused man to open the door?

"Uuughh," he groaned, getting to his feet.

He had an hour before Jack's funeral, an hour to pray for answers.

* * * *

Jason pulled to a stop in front of St. Xavier. His mouth dropped open as he spied the ambulance and police cars.

After jumping out, he raced over to where the two police officers stood.

"What's going on here?"

The younger officer held up a hand. "Who are you, sir?"

Digging in his back pocket, he glanced over their shoulders to study the crowd of men standing near the base of the bell tower. He handed his wallet to the policeman.

"I'm Jason Bentley. I own the building."

"We were about to call you. One of your stonemasons fell from the tower and broke his neck."

Jason stared at the man in shock. "You mean he's dead?"

"Yes, sir. Most people who fall from that height and break their neck don't survive."

He glared at the young officer. The older one punched his partner on the arm.

"Stop being an ass," he said before taking a step forward, hand extended. "I'm Officer Osmond. If you'll come with me, Mr. Bentley, we'll head over to talk to the men."

"Thank you," Jason replied, shaking the officer's hand.

He didn't know what to expect as Osmond escorted him over to the scene. The body still lay there. Swallowing hard, Jason looked down at the body and blinked. As horrible as the idea of the man being dead was, he realised he didn't look dead. He looked like he was sleeping, though his head was at an odd angle. Something about the man's shirt caught Jason's attention. He moved a little closer.

"Don't touch him. Once the coroner's done, we'll take him back to the morgue."

Touching the body hadn't even crossed Jason's mind. He pointed at the welts on the man's chest where his shirt had ridden up.

"What caused those?"

Osmond knelt next to him and used his pen to move the torn edge of the T-shirt aside. They stared at the three deep scratches across the stonemason's tanned skin.

"Probably caused when he lost his balance and fell."

"Is that what you think happened?" Jason glanced up at the bell tower and shook his head. "He is...*was* a professional. I can't see him taking a misstep and falling out a window."

The police officer shrugged. "It happens. I'm sure once we finish our investigation, we'll rule it an accident. We'll have to close down the construction while we gather information."

As much as Jason hated the thought of halting the renovations, he understood why it needed to be done, so he nodded and looked around for the head of the construction crew.

"Have you guys seen Hank?" he asked the electricians milling around.

"He just went back inside," one of the men said. He pointed at the main building where Hank had set up his temporary headquarters. Jason had hired as many local contractors as he could, but since he couldn't be there every day, he'd brought Hank in as his man on site.

Straightening, he frowned. "Hey, guys. You might as well head out for the day. I guess the police will need to ask you some questions, but once they're done, you can leave. Don't worry. You'll get paid your full eight."

The men mumbled, but didn't argue. Jason turned back to Osmond.

"I'm going to talk to Hank. You'll find me in the big building."

Osmond wrinkled his nose before nodding. "I'll send Thompson after you. I wouldn't go into St. Xavier, even if it was to save my life."

"Got something against abandoned monasteries, Officer?" Jason joked as he walked away.

"Only the haunted ones," Osmond replied before turning to his fellow policemen.

Jason stopped for a second, then shook it off. He had too many other things to think about to worry that a law enforcement officer considered the place haunted. He needed to talk to Hank. Entering the foyer, he glanced around and smiled.

Even though he wasn't happy about the stonemason's death, he could still appreciate the sheer size and beauty of the monastery and all the wonderful craftsmanship that had gone into building the place. He loved the old architecture. That was why he'd wanted St. Xavier the moment he'd walked through it. With the building slowly being brought back to its original glory, Jason was happier than ever that he'd taken a chance on it.

"Hank," he called.

"Back here, Jason." Hank stuck his head out from the library.

"Why weren't you out there with the others?" He headed down the hallway, dodging the construction and renovation items strewn around the area.

"I had to get our insurance papers, plus I tried calling you, but you must have your phone off."

Jason patted his pockets until he found his phone. After pulling it out, he checked it and groaned. "Sorry, the battery died, and I totally forgot to charge it on my way here."

"No problem." Hank waved in the direction of the bell tower. "I guess you saw everything anyway."

"Yeah. Officer Osmond said that we're going to have to shut down for the day, but he figured it was an accident, so we shouldn't be delayed much longer." Jason grimaced as he scrubbed his hand over his face. "Shit. Listen to me. A man died, and I sound like I care more about deadlines than I do about him."

Hank slapped him on the shoulder. "Don't worry about it. I know you're not as callous as all that, but hey, it is good news that we won't be behind."

"I told the men to go home after the police are done with them. I also let them know that they'd be paid for today, so don't dock them the time."

"That's nice of you. I'm sure they'll appreciate it."

Jason thought about what Osmond had said. "Have you heard the guys talking about the monastery?"

As they strolled back to the front, Hank appeared to think about it.

"I haven't been listening, though I do notice they seem a little on edge. I figure it's just the rumours of this place being haunted. Even the most rational and practical people get a little nervous in a place people claim has ghosts."

"Do you believe in ghosts, or that this place is haunted?" Jason propped his elbow on the intricately carved newel post at the bottom of the banister.

Hank chuckled. "If I got freaked out every time I worked someplace that was supposedly haunted, I wouldn't have a job. Ghosts don't bother me."

A bang sounded from somewhere in the monastery and he glanced up at the ceiling.

"Did you guys get the fourth floor open yet?"

"We took the door off since we couldn't get it unlocked. There are five bigger rooms up there. We think they might have been rooms for visiting clergy or the more important people who lived here. Although they're pretty badly stained in a few rooms, the floors are solid wood and should be easy to sand and refinish. The real beauty up there is the fireplaces and carved moulding along the ceilings. Very nice. Too bad you've decided to take over that floor for yourself. I'd imagine you could get a pretty penny if you put playrooms up there and charged an hourly fee to use them."

Hank winked at him and Jason grinned. When he had explained his vision to his friend, Hank had jumped on the wagon, vowing that he and his boyfriend would be some of Jason's first customers at the resort.

Although Hank's suggestion was a good one, Jason had always insisted on having his own space in his resorts. With the kind of transitory life-style he led, it was important for him to feel at home no matter where he was. "Are there any rooms ready on the second floor?"

"Sure. Come with me. Why?" Hank headed upstairs.

"I thought I would give them a once-over and take some pictures to send to Roland. He'll get the interior decorators going on designing the furniture and stuff." He held up his camera.

"Cool. Most of the rooms on the second and third floors are the same size and quality. You'll have to decide whether you want them to stay that way or if you want to knock out the walls to double their size."

Jason nodded, tugging out a notebook and a pen to jot down notes and thoughts to send to Roland. Hank talked about the stairs and the restoration needed to strengthen them, and pointed out weak spots on the walls and the ceiling.

"I made notes of them to set guys working on them, but I wanted to let you know."

"I trust you to know what needs to be done. I might stop by throughout the day, but it's not to second-guess you or to try to force you to do something my way."

"Right. I love the little suggestions you leave on my desk for me to find in the morning."

Laughing, Jason shrugged. "I don't mean to make you think I don't believe you know what you're doing. You have my number and you can tell me I'm full of shit about something if you don't like it."

Hank nodded, but didn't say anything. He directed Jason through the rooms. Jason took a lot of notes and pictures, knowing the workload he was sending off to Roland. He trusted his personal assistant could do the job.

"What are you thinking?" Hank asked as they stood at the top of the stairs.

Jason paused. "I'm thinking we should take out the walls and double the size of the rooms. It'll cut down how many guests we can have here, but we can charge more. I'll ask the architect to work something up for me with the changes." Jason snapped his notebook shut. "Show me what you've been doing with the gardens."

"We haven't come as far as we would have liked. We've been focussing our attention on the buildings and the caretaker's house at the back of the property."

"Are all the renovations finished for that?"

"Yep. It's ready for someone to move in. Maybe once the resort is open, you could use it for your manager's house instead of losing the fourth floor income. It always helps to get good workers when you offer them something like that."

Jason agreed. "I'll make sure Roland puts that in the ad when we start looking for employees for the resort."

They wandered the grounds, discussing what needed to be done and how far along they were on the schedule Jason had devised to ensure completion by opening day. By the time they had finished, all of the workers had left, and Jason said goodbye to Hank, letting the man take the rest of the day off as well. No point in making him work when the others were gone.

He sat in the middle of the gardens, on a bench the workers used for their breaks. He stared up at the building, detailing the changes that had already been made since the crews had been hired.

The windows on the fourth floor caught his attention and he studied each one. None of the panes were broken, but though the sun shone on them there didn't seem to be any light getting through. Maybe the windows were covered. He made a mental note to call Hank about them in the morning.

The hairs on the back of his neck stood up and Jason glanced around, trying to figure out why he felt like someone was watching him. He shook it off. It was probably one of the police officers examining the bell tower.

He thought about the scratches he'd spotted on the stonemason's chest. The man hadn't fallen through a window, so the glass couldn't have been the cause, yet there didn't seem to be any other explanation.

Those marks were vivid and violent, almost like there was anger behind them. They looked like claw marks from a large animal. But there weren't any around unless one of the native felines had drifted over from the Everglades, and he didn't know of any three-clawed animals that could do something like that.

"Mr. Bentley."

Jason turned to see Officer Osmond heading his way. "Yes?"

"We're done with our investigation. We're going to head out now." Osmond held out his hand. "Thank you for cooperating."

"Thank you, Officer. I'll lock up behind you."

He watched the police cars drive away as he pulled out his key chain and got ready to lock the gates. As he turned the key, instead of a clang as the tumblers engaged, Jason could have sworn he heard a scream. He froze as a shiver ran down his spine. *Shit.* Exhaustion was setting in. It came from flying across the country early that morning, then driving from the airport to the monastery. He had to be back to the airport to do it all in reverse in an hour. The fact he'd done the same routine for the past three weeks had him considering renting a house until the project was complete, but then he remembered Hank saying the caretaker's cottage was ready to live in. He could stay there. That way he would be on site in case something else happened, plus he didn't have any other projects going right then, and if Roland needed him, he could always fly home.

Pocketing the keys, he stalked to his car. When he got back to the office, he'd let Roland know he was going to stay in Florida while the monastery was being renovated. It only made sense because this resort was going to be

Jason's pièce de resistance, and he wanted everything to be perfect.

* * * *

Ryan's hands shook as he read the newspaper article about the death at St. Xavier. It was the second fatality surrounding the abandoned monastery, first Jack, and now a mason working to restore the bell tower.

Paper in hand, he sought out Father Paul. He found him in his office.

"Do you have a moment?" Ryan asked from the doorway.

Paul removed his reading glasses and set them on the blotter. "Yes. Come in."

Ryan entered the room and laid the newspaper on the priest's desk. "Have you seen this?"

Paul's jaw clenched. "I have. Terrible tragedy."

"Yes, it is." Ryan sat on the edge of the chair in front of Father Paul. "Doesn't it make you wonder if something is happening at St. Xavier? Remember, Jack Dorsel was there a few days prior to his death. His wife said he changed after appraising the place."

Paul pushed the newspaper across the desk. "It's just a coincidence."

Ryan didn't agree, but arguing with his mentor wasn't an option. Although as a Deacon he reported to Bishop Joseph Adler and not to Father Paul, Ryan had a good relationship with the older man.

Standing, Ryan picked up the newspaper. "I won't keep you."

Ryan was on his way out when Father Paul called out to him. "You're losing weight. You can't let Mr. Dorsel's death affect your health. I'll expect to see you at dinner this evening."

"Yes, Father."

Chapter Three

Holy shit! Jason shot straight up in his bed, glancing wildly around. What the hell was that noise?

There it was again. It sounded like something was beating down his door to get in. Frowning, he climbed out from under the blankets and slid on a pair of sweats he'd flung over a chair the evening before.

Jason paused in the hallway, head tilted to try and make out the sounds. Was that a scream? Had one of the elusive Florida panthers escaped the Everglades and found its way onto the property? Every atom in Jason's body hoped that was what it was because if it wasn't, someone was being murdered on the monastery grounds. Or at least that's what it sounded like.

He went to the front closet in the caretaker's cottage and opened it, pulling out the baseball bat he'd placed there a couple of days earlier. Silly really, especially if it was an animal or a robber intent on getting in. Not much a bat could do against that.

Another bang, and this time he saw the door shake with the impact. He crept up to the door and peeked out of one of the side windows. *Nothing.* What little moonlight there was shining through the cloud cover highlighted the empty front steps. He retreated back to the closet and grabbed a flashlight. Frowning, he flung open the door and stepped outside.

A light breeze danced through the trees and a heavy sensation of being watched weighed on his shoulders, like something just beyond his vision crouched and waited to see what he would do next. Taking a deep breath, Jason gripped the bat tighter and switched on the flashlight.

Nothing out of the ordinary greeted the light, though the shadows just beyond the boundary seemed to thicken. Slight tremors shook his hand, making the light quiver.

Help me. The words were brought to him on the wind. Shooting his gaze from right to left, he tried to figure out where those words had come from. He straightened his shoulders, took a deep breath to shore up his courage, and stepped off the porch onto the stone pathway. He'd never been afraid of the dark before, but after having spent three nights on the grounds of the monastery, Jason reconsidered all those legends about things that went bump in the night. For the first time in his life, he really did think there were things hiding just beyond the light in the darkest corners of the grounds.

He wound his way through the gardens, searching for the origin of the voice that still called to him from time to time. Though he knew it would be the smart thing to do, he didn't call out. Maybe he doubted what he was hearing. Maybe it was the wind teasing him by sounding like a voice as it blew through the hedges and trees. Yet there wasn't any breeze whatsoever now. The night was still, holding its breath for something to emerge from the blackness.

He huffed an exasperated sigh. God, he was losing his mind. There was nothing out there. It was all his imagination being fed by the rumours and talk amongst the workers as they renovated the buildings. Hell, one of the electricians had walked off the job two days before because he couldn't take the atmosphere anymore.

Jason went over what Hank had told him. The electrician claimed someone, or something, had watched him as he'd worked in the rooms on the fourth floor. Each time the man had looked around, there had been nobody there. He'd go downstairs for supplies and when he came back, all his tools would be scattered around whichever room he was working in.

The final straw had been when the man was leaving for the day. As he'd come to the head of the stairs leading down from the fourth floor, something had shoved him from behind, causing him to fall down several steps before catching his balance. Luckily, the electrician hadn't suffered any permanent injuries. Hank had checked him out and had sworn to Jason, after the man had left, that there were two red handprints on his back. They corroborated what he'd said about being pushed.

"Evil and sorrow haunts this place," the worker had said before he left. "You'd be wise just to let this place fall to pieces. You've awakened something by coming here and stirring up old memories."

Hank had laughed, but as Jason stood alone in the garden, staring up at the monastery, he wondered if the worker hadn't been telling the truth. Oh, he'd scoffed at the idea of spirits and ghosts haunting places, but there was an emotion hanging about the monastery. Jason couldn't put a name to it. Maybe it *was* sorrow. The realtor had informed him before he had bought the building that a tragedy had occurred there in the early sixties. She hadn't gone into a great deal of detail, but she had mentioned nuns being found dead.

He made a mental note to call Roland in the morning and ask him to research the background of St. Xavier. Suddenly he needed to know the full story. There had to be a concrete reason why the word 'sorrow' popped into his head whenever he thought of the place.

He lost track of how long he stood staring up at the imposing stone façade of the main building. There wasn't any lessening of the darkness around him, so he didn't know how close to dawn it was.

Tension seeped into his muscles as his gaze landed on the windows of the corner room on the fourth floor. Was there movement in the room? Had something just walked in front of the window?

Damn, maybe someone had broken in to steal the tools or wiring. He'd need to check it out before he called the cops. Hell, he didn't want to have them come out if it was all just his overactive imagination. He raced back to the cottage and dressed in jeans, a T-shirt, and boots. He grabbed his phone and keys as he headed out, taking the bat and flashlight as well. For some unknown reason, the electricity in the monastery had been on the fritz for the last several days. He'd had an electrician check what he could and had even called out the power company. So far no one could tell him what was causing the surges. In the end, they'd decided it would be better to cut off the main power to the building until they could determine the cause.

Help me. Please.

Shivers trickled down his spine. He ran to the side door leading from the garden into the cloister that ran the length of the building. The parquet floor always reminded him of a chessboard, and the arched ceiling gave the entire hallway a gothic feeling.

He skidded around the corner and stalked to the sweeping staircase. After flicking on his flashlight, he took the steps two at a time and got to the third floor without hearing anything else except his frantic footsteps and harsh breathing. He bent over and panted, trying to calm his heartbeat. It wouldn't pay to get up to the fourth floor and pass out because he'd deprived himself of oxygen along the way. He prided himself on keeping his body as toned and hard as it had been in his early twenties, so why did he suddenly feel like the air was being sucked from his lungs?

The hallway leading to the fourth floor door seemed darker than before. He shook his head.

"Of course, it is, jackass," he mumbled as he almost crept along the floor. "It's the middle of the night and there aren't any lights on in here."

Yet the darkness felt heavy and ponderous, coating his arms with the silt of time. Getting to the entry to the fourth floor became a test of courage for Jason. Malevolence oozed into his pores and his skin rose in gooseflesh. His hair stood on end, causing every survival instinct he had to scream at him to leave before the creature lurking in the shadows got him.

"Wait a minute," he said as he stared at the closed door.

The one thing he remembered doing the previous evening after all the workers left for the day was coming upstairs and propping the fourth floor door open. For some reason, even though they had replaced the old door with a new one, it would shut on its own and stick. They thought it had something to do with the settling of the building and the slight breezes that made their way through the enormous hallways. Here it was, shut again.

He reached out for the door knob and jerked his hand away. Heat rose from the metal, scorching his skin. *Fuck!* The building had better not be on fire or he'd just have a freaking fit. There was too much money invested in the resort venture for him to back down, even if it meant he would be way behind schedule.

After stripping off his T-shirt, he wrapped his hand in it and gripped the knob again. He could still feel the heat, but it didn't burn through the fabric. He tried opening the door, but it was stuck, just like before. Yanking on it did nothing except make his shoulders sore. In frustration, he kicked it and the door popped open.

"Just needed a little encouragement, huh?" He chuckled, despite the creepy situation.

Using the illumination from his flashlight, he made his way up the steps. For the most part, the fourth floor was sound and intact. The only real problem was the fact that large dark stains marred the floor in several of the rooms and the hallway. Jason's budget would skyrocket if they had to replace the wooden floors or put down carpet. Hank had tried everything to remove the marks, but it was like they were embedded into the very fibre of the wood. They had no idea what might have made the stains either. They were going to have a professional refinisher come in the next day or two to try and get them out.

He made his way to the large room in the northwest corner of the building. Jason had been looking at those windows in the garden earlier. It was also the room the electrician had been working in when he'd walked out, saying something kept watching him. It had been Jason's intention to use the room as his bedroom, but he was beginning to rethink that option.

As he walked, the darkness sucked him in, swallowing his light like it was a mere candle and not an industrial strength flashlight. Again, the door that had been left open was shut. There weren't any animals running around the building. Jason had had the exterminator out to get rid of all the unwanted pests. Amazingly, there hadn't been that many. Just a few stray mice and squirrels, and those were mostly on the lower floors. The fourth floor was pristine, like whoever had used those rooms had just left minutes before.

Jason pushed the door open and stepped in.

Pain like nothing he'd ever experienced hit him. Suddenly his head felt like it would implode from the pressure. He was pushed to his knees by unseen hands as unintelligible whispers spoke to him. Jason began to swat wildly at the air around him.

"Leave me alone!" he screamed.

Something slammed into his back, throwing him forward onto his stomach. His face landed in a dark, thick pool of…? *What the hell is that?* he asked himself as he tried to push himself back to a sitting position. The unseen hands continued to hold him down as the whispers grew louder.

"Find him or die," his attacker hissed.

With his face still pressed to the floor, Jason tried to determine where the voice was coming from. He gritted his teeth and rolled to his side.

In the corner of the room, caught by the bright beam of the flashlight, stood a woman. Not just any woman. It was a nun, dressed in a pure white habit, with a large gold crucifix held to her chest. Blood covered most of her skin and clothing, the splatters on her face giving the woman a crazed appearance.

Jason blinked, unsure he was seeing what was right in front of him. Despite the nun's frightening appearance, the pain in her gaze cut through him until he thought he was bleeding as much as she was.

"What do you want?" he asked. The pressure seemed to lift, and Jason pushed himself up into a sitting position.

He held out his hand to touch her, though he wasn't sure why, because he could see the painting on the wall behind her through her ethereal form. Actually he could see it through her. "What do you want?" he screamed when she continued to stare at him with tortured eyes.

"Him!"

Although the apparition's lips didn't move, Jason heard the words loud and clear. He was slammed back onto the floor, his head striking the hard wooden surface with a thud. Darkness descended over him as the nun lifted the crucifix and floated in his direction. Ice ran through his veins as he raised his hands to block the blow of the weapon she held.

* * * *

"Boss, what the hell are you doing here?"

Jason blinked, staring into the concerned face of Hank. He groaned as his crew boss helped him to sit up. Glancing around, he found himself on the floor of the corner room. His flashlight and baseball bat were scattered around him along with his phone and keys.

Shaking his head, he tried to clear his mind, grabbing his skull against the pain the movement caused. What the hell had happened last night? Had he really seen the nun? His gaze shot to the floor behind him. There was no sign of the bloody pool he'd found himself in the previous night.

Looking back up towards Hank, Jason thought quickly. Telling his construction manager the truth would only land him in the psych ward at the local hospital. "I heard noises last night and came up to investigate. I must've tripped on the door frame or something, fallen and hit my head."

Jason rubbed the lump on the back of his head.

"Shit. It's odd that you hit the back of your head when you fell, but regardless, you should get that looked at, especially if you were unconscious for long."

He took the hand Hank offered him and let the other man pull him to his feet. He felt bruised and battered, but nothing was broken. He waved off Hank's worry.

"I'll be okay. I'm going back to the cottage to clean up." He paused for a second. "Don't have anyone work up here today. I want to see about a new floor plan for this area. I'm comfortable in the cottage, so I think I'll keep it. I'll have the architect redo the layout up here. There's no sense in doing any more to it until then."

"Sure. You're the boss. Will you be okay getting back to your place?"

"Yeah. Don't worry. I'll stop back by in a little while."

When Jason got back to the cottage, he collapsed on the couch and stared into space. What the fuck had really happened? Had he truly seen a ghost, or was it just a hallucination brought on by too many nachos? He grabbed his phone from where he'd tossed it.

"*The* Bentley Corporation. Roland Harkin speaking."

"Roland, I need you to do something for me. Drop whatever you're working on now and make this your top priority."

"Okay. Is everything all right?" Roland sounded worried, and Jason realised how frazzled he still was.

"Yeah, everything's fine. I'm just curious about the background history of the monastery. Thought maybe we could merge some of it into the resort. I'm already keeping the front gate and scroll work." He leant back against the cushions and sighed, running his hand over the large goose egg on the back of his head.

"Oooh...that would be a great idea." Clicking came over the phone. "I did some initial research for you when you started looking at the property. Let me see if I can find it."

He let the silence settle between them, Roland's soft hum easing the tension from his shoulders.

"Got it. Okay, there isn't much. Saint Xavier Monastery was built in 1850 during a time when craftsmen were proud of their work. One of the few hand-carved stone buildings in the world, it was to be used as a retreat for nuns who wished to take time out of the world to focus on God." Roland grunted. "Yada yada, more history stuff. I found a snippet in the local paper about a death at the monastery but nothing else. No mention of names or anything."

"Thanks. Do a little more searching for me. I already knew about the murder. That was disclosed before I bought the place."

"Murder? It didn't say anything in the article about a murder. I know because I would've perked right up for that. You know I love that kind of mystery."

"No, I'm sure the realtor told me it was a murder. Actually, I think she said murders, plural. I think I'll head over to the local Catholic Church and see if the priests there can give me any information."

Roland snorted. "Hope lightning doesn't strike you down for entering a church."

Jason laughed. "It has been a while since I've gone, but I don't think God's interested in killing me for having the nerve to enter if He wants me to believe in Him."

"True. I'll get on that research and send you what I find. Ooh," Roland squealed. "I'm all excited now. I feel like a reporter or something."

Jason rolled his eyes. He wondered if Roland would feel the same if he'd been the one to experience the events of the previous night.

"Take care and I'll call you as soon as I find something."

"Thanks, Roland."

He closed his phone and tossed it onto the coffee table. Bracing his elbows on his knees, he covered his face with his hands and sighed. Damn, he felt like he'd been run over by a fucking semi.

Jason really needed to get cleaned up and check in with Hank before heading over to the church. Hopefully, the priests there would be able to clear up a few things for him. If not, well, maybe he'd just avoid the nachos at the local diner and pray that solved the problem of the bloody nun.

* * * *

Reaching to retrieve a wayward hymnal, Ryan was surprised when the front door of the church opened, letting light into the darkened sanctuary. "May I help you?" he asked the figure silhouetted against the sunlight.

The man stepped forward and shut the door behind him, plunging the sanctuary into shadows once more. "My name's Jason Bentley. I purchased the St. Xavier Monastery, and I was hoping there'd be someone I could talk to about a few problems I'm having?"

Mention of the monastery wasn't the only thing that suddenly had Ryan on edge. There was something about the man that called to the part of himself he'd spent a lifetime trying to deny. The tall, dark stranger couldn't have come at a worse time. Not only was Ryan functioning on little sleep, but his emotions and nerves were still raw.

"I'm sorry, Mr. Bentley, but our church suffered a tragedy recently." Ryan fought the rush of emotion that threatened. "Father Paul Burger suffered a massive stroke several days ago while getting ready for bed. Unfortunately, he passed away before help could arrive. The Bishop is working on getting us a new priest, but for now, I've been trying to hold things together."

"I'm sorry." Jason lifted his hand as if to offer Ryan comfort.

Ryan took a step back, afraid of his own response should contact be made. "Can your questions about St. Xavier wait until a replacement is named, Mr. Bentley?"

"Call me Jason, please."

Ryan nodded. "You can call me Deacon or Ryan, whichever you're more comfortable with."

Jason glanced around the church's interior. "Do you have a few moments to talk to me?"

Ryan's initial reaction was a big fat no, but he clung to his inner strength and faith. His job was to counsel and guide all people who sought his help. "Yes, but would you mind taking a walk in the rose garden?" He averted his eyes. Suddenly the church felt stifling. Whether it was the guilt of his thoughts when he set eyes on Jason, or the hours spent on his knees in prayer, Ryan didn't know. What he did know was that the man walking beside him as they stepped out into the sunshine would be his greatest test to date.

Ryan had been warned by Father Paul and Bishop Adler to ignore the events taking place surrounding St. Xavier, so he knew he was taking a chance in talking to Jason.

"Do you believe in ghosts?" Jason eventually asked after several moments of talk about the garden.

Ryan's steps faltered. He stopped and dropped to the bench. A memory suddenly blinded him to his surroundings.

A six-year-old Ryan bounded into his room and tossed his backpack onto the bed. "Charlie?" he called, kicking off his shoes.

"Who're you talking to? I told you no friends allowed in the house," his stepfather said, leaning against the doorframe.

Ryan bit his bottom lip. He knew better than to tell Joe about the man who'd become everything to him. Charlie was the only person to offer him affection since his mother had taken off. Charlie's attention wasn't always pleasant, and sometimes Ryan cried afterwards, but Charlie always stayed to hold him.

"No one," Ryan told his stepdad. He gestured to the small teddy bear he'd found in a trashcan on his way to school months earlier. "Just Charlie."

Joe glanced at the bed and shook his head. "You freak." He turned and left the room, shutting the door.

Ryan sat on the edge of the bed. He knew his friend Charlie wasn't real, just like he knew the other men and women he saw on the streets weren't real, but Charlie was all he had, and even though he couldn't hold his friend, he felt it when Charlie hugged him. It was the feeling of security he'd always longed for, and Ryan was willing to suffer the times Charlie hurt him for that warmth.

Everything had changed the day he'd been taken from his stepdad. He'd been placed in a foster home with an older woman who insisted he attend church every Sunday. In his new house there was also a man, but that man didn't hug him like Charlie had. He mostly sat and watched Lila, Ryan's foster mom, with tears in his eyes.

It was out of worry for Lila that Ryan had spoken to Bishop Adler, who had been his parish priest at the time and the man who'd helped the social worker place Ryan with Lila in the first place. Bishop Adler had been shocked to hear of Ryan's long history with unseen people. When Ryan had confessed his feelings for his old friend Charlie, the bishop had been horrified. He'd immediately placed Ryan into a special counselling programme, determined to drive out the evil he claimed had invaded an innocent boy's soul.

"Deacon?" Jason took a seat beside Ryan on the stone bench.

Ryan met Jason's gaze. Despite the years of prayer and training, he could no longer deny his feelings for his own sex, nor could he deny the truth of what he'd seen as a child. "Yes, I believe in ghosts."

* * * *

That evening, long after Jason had left, Ryan couldn't get the conversation off his mind. He paced the rectory, wishing Father Paul were still alive. The moment Jason had told Ryan about the events of the previous night, his skin had been riddled with gooseflesh. More than Jason's description, it was the haunted look in the man's hazel eyes that continued to weigh on Ryan's conscience.

Jason had asked for help from not only the Church, but from Ryan as well. Ryan sighed and sat at the large desk that had belonged to Father Paul. If he called Bishop Adler, he knew the response would be the same as the one he'd received as a young boy trying to help an older woman who had been kind to him.

Decision made, Ryan clutched his Bible to his chest and grabbed his keys. On the way to Peachtree Street, he stopped at a convenience store and picked up a few bottles of water, a disposable camera and a bag of junk food. He eyed the sack after parking the white sedan in front of St. Xavier.

Sugar had always been his drug of choice, chocolate the heroin that made him forget his problems. Ryan reached inside the bag and pulled out a Butterfinger. He slumped down in the seat, facing the imposing mansion, and peeled the yellow wrapper off the delectable treat.

Enjoying his first bite, he hummed his approval. With his eyes glued to the fourth floor of St. Xavier, Ryan settled in for what he assumed would be a long night. He made sure his camera was ready on the dashboard as he finished the first candy bar.

As he watched the house, his thoughts went to Charlie. He hadn't thought of his secret friend in years. Now that he was an adult, he understood Charlie hadn't actually been his friend at all. Instead, he'd ended up in a house haunted by a child molester. It wasn't until he'd been sent to foster care that he'd learnt the difference between the parental love he'd craved as a child and the kind of false love Charlie had offered him.

Ryan shook his head and opened the car door, abandoning his camera and sack of sugar. He walked to the tall, wrought iron fence and peered through, gripping the bars roughly in his fists. The one question he couldn't seem to answer was why he cared so much about what was inside. He was an adult. Maybe it was a chance to right the wrong that had been done to him. Maybe it was the chance to keep the nightmares away from the man he'd met earlier in the day.

The outside lights turned on, startling Ryan. He froze, expecting the bloody nun Jason had described to fly out of the house towards him.

"Ryan?" Jason's voice called from the darkness beyond the streetlight.

Ryan closed his eyes and rested his forehead on the back of his right hand. "Yeah," he returned. Remembering who he was, Ryan released his hold and straightened his jacket. "Yes," he answered again, walking down the fence line. He reached the large double gate and stopped.

Jason came into view, and Ryan's knees nearly buckled. Clothed, Jason was incredible, but with his shirt off and jeans riding low on his hips, the handsome man was a temptation like nothing Ryan had ever faced.

Jason ran his fingers through his already-mussed hair. "What're you doing out here at this time of night?"

Ryan swallowed, his mouth as dry as dirt. Regardless of his answer, he was positive he'd come off like a stalker. He stared at Jason for several moments before deciding the truth was the only way to go. "I couldn't stop thinking about what you told me. I decided to come out and..."

Ryan clamped his mouth shut. What could he say? *I came out to watch over you?*

"And?" Jason prompted, opening the gate that stood between them.

"I don't know," Ryan said with a shake of his head. "I guess…" Ryan cleared his throat. "I believe you."

The expression on Jason's handsome face was confusing. Had Ryan made him angry? "That's why you came to the church, right?"

Jason took a step back. "Would you like to come in?" he asked, gesturing to the driveway behind him. The movement highlighted Jason's muscled chest and arms.

Ryan's fingers went to the cross hidden beneath his white dress shirt. How many times in one day could his convictions be tested? "I probably shouldn't."

The corner of Jason's mouth tilted upwards in a grin that threatened Ryan's resolve. "It's the building that's scary, not me."

Ryan smiled. "I'm not sure if I agree with you." There was something about Jason that called to Ryan's baser instincts, which in turn made him uneasy. "Would it be okay if I dropped in tomorrow? I'd like a chance to talk to you further."

"Sure. I'd welcome the company. The guys I work with are great, but I'm the boss." Jason shrugged.

Taking a step in the direction of the car, Ryan gestured to the monastery. "Do me a favour and stay out of there tonight."

Jason's eyes crinkled at the corners as he chuckled. "I don't think you have to worry about that. Last night shook me up. I'm not looking for a repeat performance. At least not while I'm alone without someone to watch my back."

Ryan didn't understand his desire to be the one to watch Jason's back. It was something he needed to pray about, the main reason he needed to get into his car and go back to the rectory. Although Ryan's feet tried to rebel, he made his way towards the car. "I'll be back after my morning duties are taken care of."

"Look forward to it," Jason said, shutting the gate.

Starting the car, Ryan glanced at the sack of candy. It no longer held the appeal it once had. Unfortunately, he just might have stumbled onto something his sugar addiction couldn't replace.

Chapter Four

Ryan was surprised by a rare visit from Bishop Adler after the Tuesday morning service. Functioning on little sleep, Ryan tried to appear nonplussed by the appearance of his mentor. "Bishop Adler," he greeted with a handshake.

The bishop frowned. "Attendance seems to be down."

Ryan's hackles rose at the comment. "It's Tuesday. Only the most faithful attend services during the week."

Joseph Adler rubbed his jaw in apparent disapproval. "Are you sure you can handle your duties until Father Paul's replacement arrives?"

"When is that?" Ryan asked. He hadn't heard the Archdiocese had named a replacement.

"Father Damon Richmond will be in place by next Wednesday's service."

"Father Richmond?" Ryan had met the elderly priest on several occasions. He'd been a friend of Bishop Adler's for years.

"Is there something wrong with Father Richmond?" Joseph asked.

"No, but I thought he was retired."

The bishop nodded. "He is, but he's stepping in as a favour to me and Archbishop Ladue."

The man who had counselled Ryan since he was a boy seemed more distant than usual. Ryan hoped his wandering thoughts regarding Jason Bentley weren't visible.

"We need to discuss your ordination. Archbishop Ladue is becoming increasingly frustrated with your failure to take your vows." Joseph settled a hand on Ryan's shoulder. "You're the closest I'll ever come to having a son. If you're troubled, you can come to me."

Ryan bit the inside of his cheek. His hand moved to the coat pocket that contained one of his favourite daily treats, lemon drops. Pulling out one of the sugary candies, he stuck it into his mouth without bothering to check for lint first. Bishop Adler's feelings on homosexuality had become apparent long ago. Ryan knew discussing the reason behind his failure to commit completely to the Catholic Church would garner him condemnation instead of counselling.

Trying to change the subject, Ryan swallowed around the lump in his throat and asked about the other situation plaguing him. "Would you please tell me what you know about the St. Xavier Monastery?"

Joseph's eyebrows rose. "St. Xavier was a terrible tragedy. It was also a costly waste of the Church's time and money. Now that the Archdiocese has finally recouped some of its losses, its best we move on."

"What do you mean it was a waste? Wasn't it a sanctuary for nuns who had lost their path to God? How can the Church consider that a waste of money?"

"Because, unfortunately, the majority of them were too far off the path of a righteous life. Their Mother Superior did everything she could to no avail. They looked upon their sanctuary as a prison instead of a place of healing." Joseph turned and walked down the centre aisle of the church, obviously troubled. "One innocent in particular died because of the failed belief that people could be led back to the Church."

"One of the nuns?" Ryan asked, jumping on the clue to who was haunting St. Xavier.

"No." Joseph shook his head. "Unfortunately, one of the priests brought in to counsel the sisters was pushed down the stairs and died from his injuries."

"A priest? So there were men in the monastery?"

Joseph held up his hand. "They didn't live on the premises, but they were brought in to give sacrament and counsel. I assure you, they had only the nuns' best interests at heart."

The story didn't gel with what Ryan knew of Jason's experiences inside the building. Jason had said nothing about seeing a man on the fourth floor. "And the nuns? What happened to them?"

Joseph's back stiffened. "Dead. All of them murdered by someone they trusted. Sister Ann Cawfield." Joseph turned and walked to the door. "The important thing is that the situation was dealt with in a swift manner years ago. The Church has moved on." Joseph looked over the top of his glasses at Ryan. "And you should, too. You have more important things to attend to, like keeping your congregation together until Father Richmond is in place.

And," Joseph stressed, "planning your ordination. The time has come, Ryan."

Ryan was at a loss for words. He watched in silence as Bishop Adler walked out of the church. Yes, it was time for him to make a decision. He turned back to the altar. For years he'd prayed for the answer, a sign the life of a priest was his true calling. With Bishop Adler's patience and guidance, Ryan had come to think of the Church as home. It was the one place in the world he felt needed, and his love for God was immeasurable. When the time had come for him to attend college, Bishop Adler had suggested the seminary.

At first it had seemed like the perfect fit, but over the years Ryan had realised he preferred his quiet times of prayer over working on and offering the Gospel at mass. A monastic life was still an option, but that didn't answer his long-held questions regarding his desires of the flesh.

Ryan turned away from the altar and walked out of the side door. He immediately spotted Bishop Adler leaving the rectory with a cardboard box. "Bishop?" he called.

Joseph slowed his pace, but continued walking. He opened the trunk of his car and set the box inside. "Just a few of Father Paul's journals. I thought I'd go through them and see if they'd be of any use to Father Richmond. I'll be back to get the rest later." Before Ryan could say anything else, Bishop Adler got into his car and pulled out of the drive.

Ryan entered the rectory and immediately went to Father Paul's office. A thorough inspection showed that nothing seemed to have been disturbed. He leaned against the desk, his eyes still scanning his surroundings. With a sudden burst of energy, Ryan charged out of the office and ran up the stairs, taking them two at a time. The first thing he noticed once he reached the top was Father Paul's door, left slightly ajar. There was no doubt Bishop Adler had taken the journals from Father Paul's bedroom.

After Paul's death, Ryan had reverently cleaned the room and shut the door securely. Ryan pushed open the door, but didn't see anything out of place except... He reached the closet and turned on the light. He was surprised to discover a large bookshelf behind the hanging clothes.

Ryan examined the row of black leather books. He fingered the spines carefully before pulling one from the shelf. Inside the front cover was a year, written in Father Paul's handwriting, 2005. Sliding the journal back into place, he pulled another from further down the row, 1981. How long had Father Paul been keeping them?

It was obvious by the thin line of dust at the edge of the top shelf that it had been cleared recently. Ryan removed the first book from the second shelf, 1969. Journal in hand, Ryan sank to the floor. If the books were in chronological order, the journals Bishop Adler had taken were for the years prior to nineteen-sixty-nine.

"What use would Father Raymond have for journals that old?" Ryan asked aloud. He began scanning the pages, trying to understand. From what he could tell, the journals were personal in nature. He closed the book and put it back on the shelf, feeling guilty.

Ryan's cell phone rang, making him jump. He fished the phone out of his pocket. "Hello?"

"Ryan?"

Ryan smiled at the deep timbre of Jason's voice. "Yes?"

"I wondered if you were free for lunch."

Ryan glanced at his watch, surprised to see that it was almost eleven-thirty. The idea of seeing Jason pleased him more than the thought of lunch. "I could do that. Do you have any place special in mind?"

"Not really. I figure you know more about the area than I do," Jason answered.

"The best place in town for lunch is Arnie's Sub Shoppe, but it's take-out only. I could swing by and pick up a couple of sandwiches and meet you somewhere."

"Sounds good. Meet me here at the jobsite. I like anything with roast beef as the main ingredient."

Ryan smiled. "I'll be there in thirty minutes." He hung up the phone and pulled himself to his feet. After turning off the light and shutting Father Paul's door, Ryan raced to get ready. He took off his black suit coat and dress shirt, replacing them with a sedate white golf shirt. His excitement to see Jason continued to grow as he made sure his dark auburn hair was smoothed down instead of sticking up at odd angles as it had a tendency to do.

Climbing into his car, the butterflies in Ryan's stomach seemed to take flight. He gripped the steering wheel and closed his eyes. Like a bolt of lightning, the truth of the situation hit him. It didn't matter that he barely knew Jason. The fact that he wanted to be with him was enough to shake Ryan to his core. How did he reconcile his desires with his beliefs? Would God turn his back on him?

* * * *

A knock on the driver's window got Ryan's attention. He turned to stare into Jason's big, hazel eyes.

"Are you okay?" Jason asked through the glass.

Ryan blinked several times before rolling down the window. "What're you doing here?"

"It's almost two. I got worried." Jason opened the car door and squatted in front of Ryan. "You seemed pretty out of it when I pulled up. Is something wrong?"

Ryan nodded his head. With his decision made, his entire life had been turned on end. The honest concerned expression on Jason's handsome face made Ryan feel better about his choice. "Can we go somewhere and talk?"

"Sure." Jason gestured at the rectory. "You want to go inside?"

"No!" Ryan blurted out. "I can't…"

"Okay. Okay," Jason said again in a soothing manner. He stepped back and held out his hand. "We can go to my place."

Ryan nodded and took the offered hand. The fact that he welcomed the refuge the grounds of the haunted monastery offered said a lot for his mental state. Although Ryan was honest enough to admit it could have something to do with his desire to be with Jason.

Jason led Ryan to a silver Jaguar and opened the door. Ryan climbed in and reached for the seatbelt while Jason walked back to Ryan's generic-looking sedan. Ryan's eyes scanned the luxurious interior in awe. The car seemed equipped with every bell and whistle imaginable.

Jason opened the door and got in, handing Ryan's keys over. "I locked it."

Ryan hadn't even realised he'd left the keys in the ignition. "Thanks." He searched for something else to say as Jason pulled away from the kerb. "This is a beautiful car."

Jason grinned and nodded, running a hand over the leather dashboard. "Thanks. I just got it. When I only came to town for a few days a week, I just used rentals, but now that I guess I'll be staying a while, I decided it would be better to just lease one."

Ryan nodded. He tried to keep his eyes to the front, but they began to wander to the man driving the car. When it came to talking to a man he was interested in pursuing, Ryan was a complete and total virgin.

"So what's going on?" Jason asked.

The truth clung to the tip of Ryan's tongue. How did you tell a man you couldn't stop thinking about him? "I don't think I'm meant to become a priest," he finally said.

The car slowed as Jason drove through the monastery gates. "That's a pretty big decision."

"Yeah," Ryan agreed. "It's been a long time coming. I've put off taking my vows for too long, trying to figure out my feelings."

"Can I ask?"

Ryan opened his mouth to answer, but his emotions threatened to overwhelm him. He shook his head and took a deep breath as Jason pulled up to a house to the side of the property.

Jason put the car in park and reached over to lay a hand on Ryan's shoulder. "That's okay. We don't have to talk about it."

When Jason started to remove his hand, Ryan reached out and grabbed it. "Right now, I think you're the only one I can talk to."

Jason threaded his fingers through Ryan's. "Okay. Let's go inside, and I'll order a pizza. If you feel like talking after we've filled our stomachs, I'm more than happy to listen."

"I'm sorry I forgot about our sandwiches." Ryan stared at their intertwined hands. It was the first time in his life that he'd touched a person out of desire. He rubbed his thumb across Jason's sun-bronzed skin. Ryan waited for the guilt to besiege him but none came. "I like you," he whispered.

Jason turned in the seat and used his free hand to cup Ryan's cheek. "I won't lie and tell you the attraction isn't there because I've had a hard time keeping you off my mind. But being someone's guinea pig isn't something I'm interested in."

Guinea pig? "No. The decision's already been made. I'd never use you like that. I was just trying to be honest with you."

Before Jason could reply, someone was at his window. "Jason, we've got another problem."

Jason released Ryan and opened his door. "What's going on?"

"Those stains on the fourth floor?" the man began.

"Yeah," Jason answered, gesturing for Ryan to get out of the car.

"The refinisher's here. He said the stains go all the way through the wood in the corner room."

Jason glanced over his shoulder and beckoned Ryan to his side. "Ryan, this is Hank, my contractor."

"Nice to meet you." Ryan shook Hank's hand.

"You want to go with us to take a look at the floor?" Jason asked.

Ryan looked up at the imposing grey building. A woman staring down at him from one of the windows confirmed what he'd already known. "I'd rather take a tour later once the workmen have gone for the day."

Jason's head tilted to the side. "Will you be okay down here for a few minutes?"

"Sure. I'll call and order that pizza. Is one with everything okay with you?"

"Sounds good." Jason smiled before walking off with Hank at his side.

Ryan dug in his pocket and pulled out his phone. He was thankful for the reprieve. It would give him time to get his thoughts in order.

* * * *

As Jason followed Hank into the monastery and upstairs, he couldn't get his mind off Ryan. Having known the man for only a day, he shouldn't be as invested in Ryan's life as he seemed to be. All he'd thought about the previous night was the young deacon and how disappointed he'd been when he realised Ryan was going to commit his life to God.

Surprise and sudden guilt had hit him when Ryan had told him he wasn't going to be a priest. Why he thought he had any influence over the guy's decision was beyond him. It wasn't like they'd known each other for a long time. The deacon said he'd been thinking about whether or not to take his vows for a while, and maybe Jason's entrance into his life made him realise it would never work for him.

Jason paused at one of the windows overlooking the driveway. He saw Ryan leaning against his car with his phone pressed to his ear. If any of the priests at Jason's childhood church had looked like Ryan, Jason probably would have gone more often to stare at them, not to listen to the sermons. After years of hearing how he was an abomination, he had decided to cut his losses and risk going to hell for being gay.

He'd never understood how priests and nuns could stay celibate. Sex was a natural way of life, and it seemed to

Jason that if God didn't want people to have sex, He shouldn't have made it so awesome.

"Boss, are you coming?"

Turning, Jason glanced up at Hank. "Yeah."

The door leading up to the fourth floor was propped open again, but this time someone used a steel rod instead of a piece of wood.

"Have we figured out why this door keeps closing? I can't think that the building has settled so much that the door won't stay open. The windows are being updated, so there shouldn't be a cross-breeze coming through from upstairs either."

Hank shrugged. "All of the architects, engineers, and construction guys have checked it out. Can't find anything wrong with it. Figured the steel would keep the door from shutting, because it's a pain to get it open once it happens."

"Tell me about it," Jason muttered. As he passed through the doorway and up the steps, he turned back to the door which seemed to give a slight groan. The effect on his skin was immediate. Jason glanced at the raised goose flesh on his arms and shook his head. "Since I've decided to stay put in the caretaker's cottage, I don't really need the security the door provides. Take the damn thing off its hinges and leave it off. Other than heating and cooling purposes, I don't see the need for it anymore. Hell, I'll just count on my bills being higher if it'll keep my guests from being trapped up here."

"Thanks. That's the decision I'd hoped you'd reach," Hank said, waiting at the top of the stairs.

The refinisher knelt in the hallway at the spot of one of those mysterious stains. He looked up as they approached, and Jason didn't like the concerned expression on the man's face.

"Hank says you can't do anything about the stains. The ones you sanded down on the other floors came out great, so what's the problem up here?"

The guy climbed to his feet and brushed his hands off on his jeans before shaking Jason's hand. "Actually, most of the stains I can get rid of. At least the ones in the hallway and some of the other rooms. It's the stain in the corner office and the one at the bottom of the stairs I can't do anything about."

"Bottom of the stairs?" Jason shot Hank a questioning look. "I didn't know there was one."

Hank seemed surprised as well. "I don't remember seeing one."

They all trooped down the stairs again, and the refinisher studied the wood floor about a foot from the last step. His puzzled frown alerted Jason that something odd had happened.

"Now that's strange. When I got upstairs this morning, there was a pretty large stain right here." He pointed to the place. "It's gone now."

"Maybe you're mistaken. Maybe you're thinking of a spot on the fourth floor," Hank suggested.

"No. I remember it being right here because I thought it looked like something spilled right there. I figured someone let whatever it was set long enough to stain." The guy rubbed his chin and shook his head. "Oh well, it might have been a wet spot that dried. Now let's discuss that stain in the corner office."

As they ascended the stairs once more, Jason shuddered as a bone-chilling wave of air washed over him, pouring from the top of the staircase towards the third floor. He fought the urge to turn and run from the building. Whatever was happening in St. Xavier, Jason wasn't going to run away. He'd face it the best he could and get to the bottom of it.

As much as he hated to think that his newest acquisition was haunted, he was beginning to get that impression. Ryan's church held the key to finding out why, yet Jason had the feeling it would be very difficult to get the church to divulge what had really happened at the monastery so long ago.

"Did someone leave a window open up here?" Hank shivered, rubbing his hands up and down his arms. "I didn't think it was that cold outside, but maybe there's a storm moving in."

"I didn't see any windows open when I did my walk-through," the refinisher answered.

Jason stalked to the corner office and pushed open the door. It took everything he had to set foot in the room. He walked over to stained wood floor and let out a soft gasp. Taking a quick glance over his shoulder, he saw Hank and the refinisher stop just outside the door to talk about the floor there.

Jason bent over and picked up the small, gold wedding band. He knew for a fact the ring hadn't been there before. It was too small to be a man's ring so it obviously wasn't one of the workers' or the refinisher's. Had the bloody nun dropped it? Was that even possible? He slipped it into his pocket before Hank or the refinisher could see it. He'd have Ryan look at it when they got to the cottage.

"See this stain?"

Jason nodded as he looked at the spot where the other two stood. "And it's too deep for you to get out?"

"There's no way to get out. It's soaked right into the wood, so far down that you're better off removing it and putting new stuff down. Same with the one you're standing next to."

Jason gritted his teeth. With each new development, his budget rose. The unfortunate thing was he'd already sunk so much of his money into the place, he couldn't pull out of the project without losing his shirt.

"But you think you can get the stains out from the rest of the wood on this floor?" He pulled out his phone and started dialling headquarters.

The refinisher nodded. "Those shouldn't be a problem. They aren't as deep."

"What do you think made them? There wasn't any structural damage to the roof, so it couldn't have been water." Hank squatted down and ran a finger along the edge of the stain. "It's so dark. I've never seen anything like that."

Jason stared down at the dark stain. It was more than three feet at its widest spot and the edges were ragged. He blinked and the spot almost seemed to glisten like it was still fresh and wet. He was about to bend down and touch it when Roland answered the phone.

"*The* Bentley Corporation."

Jason blinked again, and the stain went back to being dry and faded. "Roland, we're going to have to readjust the budget again."

"Shit. Again? What is it this time? You want to give the landscapers more money to keep them from walking off the job like the others?" Roland groused, but Jason heard the clicking of keys over the phone.

Jason wandered over to the window that overlooked the front of the house. He saw that Ryan no longer stood by the car. Frowning, Jason moved to the other window and spied Ryan sitting on a bench in the garden, bracing his elbows on his knees as he leant forward to stare at the ground.

"Jason?" Roland prompted.

"Huh?" He refocused on his conversation. "Oh, the refinisher for the floors says he can't do anything about a couple of stains on the fourth floor. Guess we're going to have to replace it which, of course, costs more money. Thank God, he can get the rest of the floors done."

At the word 'God', the air around Jason dropped at least five degrees. He double-checked the window, even though he knew it wasn't open. His face tingled like cobwebs brushed against it, and he lifted his hands to scrub them away.

"Idiot," he muttered even as he did it.

There weren't any cobwebs anywhere in the monastery. The construction crew had cleaned it from top to bottom while checking the structural integrity of the building.

"What?"

"No, not you. I was thinking about something else."

Ryan chose to look up right at that moment, like he knew Jason was watching him. Jason smiled and started to raise his hand, but Ryan's eyes widened and even from a distance, Jason could see fear fill the man's face.

What the hell? Jason glanced to his right and left. No one and nothing stood beside him, though there was a definite cold spot to his right where he'd felt the 'cobwebs' earlier. Christ, he had to get a grip on this whole thing. Something had to be done to figure out what was happening at St. Xavier. He couldn't let ghosts or spirits bring his dream to a halt.

"Okay. I'm faxing you the new budget. We haven't reached the cut-off point you agreed to spend on the resort, but we're getting close. Try not to find other expensive problems." Roland sighed. "Have you been working the entire time you've been out there? Please, tell me you found some hunky construction worker to keep you warm at night."

Jason looked over his shoulder to see Hank and the other guy had moved further away from him. "Not a construction worker, but possibly a former priest."

"Priest?"

Jason held the phone away from his ear as Roland squealed.

"You do realise that it's like a sexual fantasy to corrupt a man of the cloth, right? Have you kissed him yet? Or better yet, have you slept with him?"

"No. No. And no. Technically, he was never a priest, just about to become one. And I just met him yesterday. I'm not that fast a worker."

Roland giggled. "Honey, you do work that fast when you want sex. I've seen you at the clubs."

Blushing, Jason agreed. "You're right about that. But he's pretty innocent, I think, and I'm not going to cause him to stray."

"I thought you said he wasn't technically a priest," Roland commented.

"I'm not going to discuss this with you, Roland. Go earn that outrageous salary I pay you." He hung up before Roland could say anything else.

He stuffed his phone into his pocket and stared down at Ryan, who had started waving like mad. Jason pressed his hand to the window in return. Ryan shook his head and motioned for Jason to come down. Suddenly Jason felt an overwhelming need to get out of the oppressive room and run down to be with Ryan.

"Hank, you have my permission for the new floor in here." Jason nodded at the refinisher. "You can do your job. I trust that you'll be able to get the rest of it off."

"Yes, sir." Both men said at the same time.

Jason rushed from the room and down the stairs. As his foot hit the exact area the refinisher had said there'd been a spot earlier, he skidded across the floor like he'd hit a patch of oil.

"Fuck," he shouted while pinwheeling his arms to keep his balance. He hit the wall and bounced back slightly.

"Are you okay, boss?" Hank yelled down to him.

"Yeah, just tripped." He wasn't about to tell Hank what had really happened, considering Jason wasn't sure what *had* happened.

There was nothing there. No stain and nothing slick or wet that could have caused him to slip. The corridor was light enough for him to check the bottom of his shoe. Nothing there either.

"What the fuck just happened?" he whispered to himself as he continued downstairs and out of the side door.

Once in the garden, the overwhelming anger and fear he hadn't even been aware of feeling lifted from him. He joined Ryan on the bench and studied the window where he'd been standing a few minutes earlier.

"Something very strange is happening," he admitted.

Out of the corner of his eye, he saw Ryan nod. "I would have to agree with you there."

"What did you see standing next to me?"

Ryan opened his mouth and Jason took the man's hand.

"Don't lie or deny you saw something. I could see the look on your face and I felt something while I stood there."

Ryan stared at their linked hands. "I saw a woman, a nun, probably *the* nun. The front of her tunic was stained red."

"The bloody nun. Damn, who is she and why is she haunting that room? I haven't felt her anywhere else. Oh, and now it appears I have a vanishing stain on my hands as well."

Jason rubbed his thumb over Ryan's knuckles while he thought.

"A vanishing stain?" Ryan sounded breathless.

"Yeah. There's a spot at the bottom of the stairs leading up to the fourth floor. Or at least there was one earlier today when the refinisher got here. When we went up, it was gone. As I was coming back downstairs, I skidded across the same damn place like it was wet or slick with something. Yet when I looked back, it was gone and I don't have anything on the bottom of my shoes."

Jason shook his head. As beautiful as St. Xavier was, he couldn't help feeling that everyone might be better off if the place was bulldozed to the ground.

"I have some information I should tell you."

The pizza delivery guy picked that exact moment to show up. Jason stood and pulled Ryan to his feet.

"Let's grab the pizza and go to my place. You can tell me everything and anything you want after we eat. I'm getting the feeling I'm going to need all the strength I have to survive the restoration of this place."

"Okay."

They headed towards the driveway. A burning sensation settled between Jason's shoulder blades like someone who hated him was staring at him. He glanced over his shoulder at the fourth floor. There was a dark shape standing in one of the windows and Jason knew the malevolent emotions came from it.

It was definitely time to retreat and regroup. He peeked at Ryan's plump lips and decided to add another 'r' to the list. Relax. Kissing Ryan sounded like a great way to achieve relaxation. He paid for the pizza and led the way to his cottage, not sure if he rushed out of eagerness to be alone with Ryan or to be away from the evil brimming in the monastery.

Chapter Five

Ryan was very aware of Jason's proximity as they ate their lunch on the sofa. Chewing a bite of the greasy pizza, he caught Jason staring. "What?"

Jason lifted his napkin and dabbed the corner of Ryan's mouth. "Tomato sauce," Jason explained, dropping the napkin but not his hand. His large, calloused thumb rubbed over Ryan's bottom lip. "I know I'll probably go to hell for this, but I want to kiss you so bad I can't think of anything else."

Ryan felt the blush creep up his neck. With his pale skin, it was impossible to hide the effect Jason's words had. "It probably isn't a good idea," he whispered as Jason's thumb continued to tempt him. Ryan shocked himself by leaning into Jason.

Jason's hand moved to the back of Ryan's neck as he closed the distance between them. Ryan held his breath when Jason's lips pressed against his. Paralysed by the overwhelming sensations coursing through his body, he gasped when he felt Jason's tongue skim across his lips. Ryan was neither naïve nor ill-informed. He'd seen movies where men and women kissed, and he knew where it usually led.

Jason seemed to be handling Ryan with care, but Ryan wasn't sure he was ready for more. Although his body was definitely ready. The filling of his cock was testament to Ryan's need, but it was like jumping off a cliff. Ryan realised he'd prefer to be lowered down slowly.

Ryan pulled out of the kiss and stared into Jason's eyes. What should he say? 'Thank you' seemed inadequate. If he asked to slow down would Jason misinterpret his desire? "That was nice," he finally said.

"Better than nice," Jason agreed with a charming grin. "Did I make you uncomfortable?"

With a shrug, Ryan tried to put his feelings into words. Being honest would be the right thing to do, but would Jason shy away from him? "Not really. That was my first real kiss. Although I've made my decision, I think it'll be a while before I feel comfortable taking the path I've chosen."

Jason seemed to study Ryan for several moments before speaking. "What made you change your mind about becoming a priest?"

"You," Ryan said simply.

Jason immediately shook his head. "Although I'm incredibly flattered, I don't want to carry that kind of responsibility."

Ryan realised Jason had misunderstood him. "No. I didn't mean you specifically. After meeting you yesterday, I haven't been able to get certain things off my mind. My desire for men has been a part of me since I was a teenager. I was told it was wrong, and that the only reason

I felt the way I did was because of experiences I suffered at an early age. I believed that, or at least tried to, for many years. But meeting you, desiring you, has nothing to do with Charlie. I finally understood that."

Ryan placed his hand on his chest. "I can't commit my heart, and my life, to God, knowing I have these desires."

"Who's Charlie?" Jason asked.

Ryan looked in the direction of the monastery. Even though he couldn't see the imposing structure from where he sat, he still felt its presence. "Charlie was a ghost." He went on to tell Jason about the two years he'd spent believing Charlie truly loved him like a father would. "Even though I know the truth about what Charlie really was, at the time I believed I needed him in my life."

"Where was your mother when all this was going on?"

"I don't know. She ran off just before Charlie appeared, leaving me with my stepfather. He didn't want me, but he needed the food stamps taking care of me provided."

Jason brushed the back of his hand down Ryan's cheek. "Being with a real man who desires you is nothing like being abused at the hands of an evil spirit. You know that, right?"

"My mind does. It's my heart that I'm still trying to convince."

Jason nodded and reached for another slice of pizza. "No pressure. I think we both have plenty on our plates. It'd be smart for both of us to take things slow."

Thankful for the change in topic, Ryan decided to tell Jason what he knew about the monastery. "A man, a priest, died in the monastery."

"Where?" Jason asked, dropping the pizza.

"Bishop Adler told me he was pushed down the stairs by one of the nuns. I have a feeling we both know exactly where." Ryan watched as gooseflesh broke out on Jason's skin.

"I've ordered the door to the fourth floor removed, but maybe I should reconsider and have the whole floor sealed off."

Ryan swallowed around the newly-formed lump in his throat. The thought of confronting what roamed the monastery scared him, but what else could he do? The building had housed nuns. It was obvious by the stories Jason told that at least one of them needed someone's help. Although Ryan couldn't commit his heart to God, he owed it to his Lord to help his children rest in peace.

"Sealing the door isn't the answer. There's obviously at least one spirit trapped inside the building. I don't expect you to understand, but I have to help them cross over. I'd like to go in as soon as the workmen leave for the day." He glanced at Jason. Here was the hard part, trying to convince Jason that he wasn't completely crazy. "I'm not sure if it's because I've always believed in ghosts or what, but I can usually see them."

Jason took the statement better than Ryan had hoped. "Can you communicate with them?" Jason asked.

"Not since Charlie. And it seems I can only see ghosts that I have a connection to. I've occasionally witnessed a deceased member of the congregation sitting beside the surviving spouse during their funeral. They don't usually stay long, but I see them." Unconsciously, Ryan began scratching at the inside of his wrist. "How could I have been so stupid to think it was love that Charlie was offering?" He looked up at Jason. "But I did. I honestly thought Charlie was trying to make up for what my parents didn't give me." It wasn't until Jason covered

Ryan's hand that he realised he'd scratched a nasty path into his own skin.

Staring at the red welts, a memory assaulted him. It had been the last time he'd seen Charlie before Ryan was put into foster care.

"Why're you doing this?" a young Ryan asked his stepfather. He struggled against the ropes that tied him to his bed. The coarse texture of his bindings rubbed at his skin, making it red and raw.

"You've got the demon inside of you, boy." Joe stepped back, his eyes wild.

Ryan stared up at his stepfather. Shame filled him as he realised Joe had witnessed Charlie's nightly expression of love. "It's not what you think."

"Writhing on the bed like a dog in heat isn't natural for a boy your age." Joe shook his head, running his stubby fingers through the mass of greasy brown hair. "I gotta figure out what to do with you. I need that money. Hell!" Joe yelled, turning to slam his fist into the wall.

As Ryan watched in silence, Charlie appeared in the room and moved towards Joe. Faced with a choice, Ryan stared at the two men. One had given him love, the other only pain and disdain. "Charlie," he whispered, getting the ghost's attention.

"What'd you say?" Joe snarled.

Ryan ignored his stepfather and made eye contact with his friend. The anger evident on Charlie's face worried Ryan. It would take a single word from him and Charlie would let loose his fury on Joe. "Don't hurt him, Charlie. I just need to get free."

"He's mean to you," Charlie countered in a voice only Ryan could hear. "He deserves to suffer."

Ryan shook his head. "No one deserves to suffer."

"You're fucking crazy," Joe said, taking a step in the direction of the open door.

Before Ryan had a chance to call a warning, Charlie had slammed the door, blocking Joe's exit. Joe reached for the knob as his face was smashed into the door.

"Charlie!" Ryan called, struggling to get out of his bindings. "Please. They'll blame me."

With a transparent grip still on the back of Joe's head, Charlie looked towards Ryan. "You're mine. He's not allowed anywhere near you."

Within the span of a single heartbeat, Ryan's world came crashing down. Charlie didn't love him. The ghost he'd considered his only friend thought of Ryan as a possession. "I thought you cared for me, but you don't, do you?"

It was Charlie's turn to look at Ryan as if he were crazy. "You're the only person I do care about. I'm trying to show you how much by taking care of this piece of trash." Charlie slammed Joe into the door once again.

Tears clouded Ryan's vision as the truth was laid out in front of him. "Go. Just leave me alone."

Joe slumped to the floor as Charlie released him and floated towards Ryan. "I can't go anywhere. I'm still here. I've been here for over thirty-six years." Despite his earlier anger, Charlie appeared saddened by what he was telling Ryan.

"What do you mean?"

"They buried me under the back porch."

"Who did?" Ryan asked.

"The fathers of some of the boys I was friends with. No one cared that I vanished. The police never came." Charlie reached out and touched Ryan's cheek. "You were the only person who ever cared."

Ryan swallowed around the lump in his throat. "Did you hurt those boys?"

Charlie shook his head. "I only tried to love them, to have them love me."

Although Ryan was young, he understood what Charlie was, but he also understood mental illness when he saw it. "Let me go, and I'll tell the police where you're buried."

"I can't do that."

"You have to. If you love me you have to let me go." Ryan looked at his bleeding wrists. "I'm hurting, Charlie."

The bonds holding Ryan fell from his wrists. Ryan sat up and looked around the room. There was no sign of Charlie. Maybe he'd been wrong. In his own, twisted way, maybe Charlie really had loved him.

"Are you with me?" Jason asked, leaning over Ryan.

Ryan blinked several times. He was lying on the couch, flat on his back. "What happened?"

"I don't know. We were talking and then you scratched yourself. Next thing I knew your eyes rolled back into your head and you fainted. I was about a minute away from calling for an ambulance when you started to wake up."

Ryan rubbed his eyes and pushed himself into a sitting position. Telling Jason about his recollections didn't feel right. Ryan couldn't believe he'd forgotten the day he'd escaped from his stepfather's house and had run to the police. He'd explained to the authorities there was a man buried under the porch. They hadn't believed him at first, but then they got it into their heads that Ryan's stepfather had killed someone and Ryan was trying to cover for him.

They had taken Ryan's bloody and battered stepfather away before investigating the large area under the back porch. Several days after being placed in his new foster home, Ryan had seen the front page of the local newspaper. After the body had been found, the questions had begun, most of them centring on Ryan and how he knew about Charles Lundgren's murder.

It was Bishop Adler who had finally stepped in at the request of Ryan's foster mother, Lila. After Bishop Adler calmed the police, Ryan had felt more comfortable telling Bishop Adler about the man who had watched Lillian with such sadness.

"I'm okay," he finally told Jason. "I haven't been getting much sleep lately. Guess it finally caught up with me."

Jason left the room and came back with a glass of water and three pain relievers. "Here. Why don't you take a nap? You've still got a couple of hours before the guys call it a day."

Ryan wasn't tired, but he had some thinking to do. "Thanks. I think I'll take you up on that offer."

Jason helped Ryan stand and led him in the direction of the master bedroom. "I have a few phone calls to make, but if you wake up and I'm not around, you'll likely find me at the job site."

Ryan reached out and grabbed Jason's hand. "Please stay out of the building until I have a look around."

Jason squeezed Ryan's hand. "Okay. Believe me, after what happened earlier, I'm in no rush to go back inside."

"Good." Ryan took off his shoes and settled on Jason's bed, pleased when Jason covered him with a spare quilt. He closed his eyes and waited for Jason to leave the room before rolling onto his back. How far was he willing to go to release the nun from the monastery?

* * * *

Jason checked on Ryan a few minutes later and noticed the younger man was out like a light. He tucked the blanket around Ryan's shoulders before leaving and heading to the living room. Flopping on to the couch, he

80

thought about calling Roland, but there were some things a man should research on his own, and the person who could be his new love interest was one of them. Jason did have work to do though, and needed to get it done before he went digging into Ryan's past.

Next time he looked at his watch, an hour had gone by, and it didn't look like Ryan was ready to stir yet, so Jason decided it was time to do a little background check on the deacon. He opened a new window on his internet browser and typed in Ryan Christopher.

Several Ryan Christophers popped up, and Jason shook his head. Obviously, he needed to tighten his search. What was the name Ryan had muttered when he'd freaked out on him earlier? Charlie Lundgren. That was it.

He typed in Charlie's name and a couple of links came up, but Jason was interested in only one. It was a newspaper article dated fourteen years earlier, and from Jason's estimation, Ryan was twenty-five, so it would put him at the right age for it.

Clicking on the link, he waited for the page to load. What had happened to Ryan all those years ago that would create such a reaction in him? The man had scratched his wrist and something told Jason it wasn't the first time the deacon had inflicted that particular injury on himself.

Jason read the headline. "Missing Man's Body Found." He scrolled down and read the article about how a local man, Charlie Lundgren, had been missing for over thirty years until a ten-year-old boy appeared to tell them about the body buried under the porch at his house.

Jason shook his head as he read how Ryan and his stepfather had been hounded by not only the media but the police department as well.

Reading further, he noticed the Catholic Church had stepped in to protect Ryan from any further questions. Father Alder had taken the young boy under his wing and placed him with an elderly member of his congregation, which would explain why Ryan had stayed in the church for so long. He felt obligated to make the bishop proud.

Jason rolled his eyes. Ryan's decision had to be more complicated than simply feeling grateful to the bishop for protecting him. A person didn't come to the point of dedicating his entire life to God because he wanted to repay a favour. That went to the extreme.

No, Ryan believed strongly in his God and religion, but now he was going to turn his back on that because of his attraction to Jason. Not good. He didn't want to be responsible for Ryan changing his mind. He didn't want the weight of that choice on his shoulders.

Ryan had told Jason he'd thought about his ordination for a long time and kept putting it off because of his doubts. Would Ryan have gone through with it if Jason hadn't shown up at his church?

Jason shut the browser down and set his laptop aside. After standing, he paced the room from the couch to the window. He paused to stare out of the window up at the monastery and a shiver chased down his back. There was something wrong in that building, yet how could he go about proving it to anyone besides Ryan? Should he say anything to the rest of his crew or try to deal with it using Ryan's experience with ghosts?

Christ! His mind returned to Ryan and the kiss they'd shared. It had been a long time since Jason had kissed a virgin. He confessed to himself that he enjoyed knowing he would be Ryan's first, if they got that far. Maybe when their situation was fixed, Ryan would come to his senses and realise he was throwing away all of his training by following the attraction between them.

Shaking his head, Jason chuckled. Wasn't it slightly arrogant of him to assume he could effect such a change in Ryan? He wasn't ignorant about his own looks and personality, but he didn't think he was all that and a bag of chips. No, Ryan's attraction might simply come from being close to another gay man, one he didn't have to hide around.

He dropped to the bench in front of the big bay window facing the monastery. After drawing his knees up, he rested his chin on them and stared out into the garden. How difficult must it be to have to hide a fundamental part of yourself?

Jason had been lucky. As soon as he'd realised he was gay, he had come out to his family. Of course, at that time, his family consisted only of his sister. His father and mother had died by then. His sister was as supportive as she could be, trying to keep them together and finish school as well. He'd kept his mouth shut during school, knowing how dangerous it could be for him in a small mining town to be out.

But the moment he hit college, he'd gone wild, experimenting with all the things he'd never had a chance to try in high school. By the time he graduated, he'd sown his wild oats and settled down for the most part. He still had more than his fair share of one-night stands, but his life didn't lend itself to a serious relationship at the moment.

Jason spent more days travelling than he did at home. It made having a boyfriend difficult, unless said man could travel along with him. Also, with all his money and success, sometimes it was hard to know for sure if they were interested in him or his possessions. Sometimes, late at night, he wished he could find someone who would like him for himself, not his bank account.

He leant his forehead on the cool glass and snorted softly. Listen to him whine about how lonely he was. He had everything he wanted; money, an interesting job, and good friends. His sister still loved him, and while they didn't see each other often, they did talk as much as they could with the lives they led.

His phone rang, and he jumped to his feet, happy to leave those thoughts behind. He snatched his phone off the coffee table and punched the talk button.

"Yes, Roland?"

"Hey boss man, how are things going down there?"

Jason smiled at Roland's bright greeting. "It's going as well as can be expected. God knows every time I turn around, I'm spending more money."

He shook his head as Roland chuckled.

"That's what happens when you buy an enormous building that hasn't been used for years. You couldn't just buy some land and build something new. No, you had to have atmosphere and shit." Roland grunted.

"Did you want something or did you just call to yank my chain?"

Shuffling and clicking came over the phone, so Jason assumed Roland either had information or more questions about the project.

"I wanted to let you know I did a little more digging into St. Xavier. Seems it used to be a retreat for wayward nuns."

"Wayward nuns? Like Maria from *The Sound of Music* wayward or what?"

"Not sure." Roland muttered something under his breath before continuing, "I think it was more those who had turned from God for various reasons. Probably couldn't take that celibate vow anymore. Goodness knows I would never agree to that. I mean really, what's the point of life without fucking?"

Jason flopped down on the couch and tilted his head back to stare at the ceiling. "I'm with you, Roland, but there is such a thing as believing so much in your calling that you'll give up everything for it."

"Hmmm…" Roland didn't sound convinced. "Whatever. Anyway, the monastery closed down after some nasty murder business. I couldn't get all the details because either newspapers back in the sixties just really sucked or someone shut the story up before it could get out. So screw them. I've got a call into the local librarian there in town. Hopefully she'll be able to fill in the missing bits. Librarians are always the best for hometown gossip. Oh, crap, I almost forgot. It didn't say so in the newspaper article, but I think a priest might have either died at the monastery or right after all the shit went down there because just below the article was another one about a big funeral service for one of the local Catholic priests. It didn't list a cause of death, but once again, it could have something to do with the lack of sleaze reporting back then."

"Ryan already told me there was a priest killed in the monastery."

"Ryan? Would this be that almost priest you made mention of last time we talked?"

He never should have said anything about Ryan to Roland. "Yes, and I'm not telling you anything. Mostly because nothing has happened and you better not discuss this with the other personal assistants. My love life isn't grist for the gossip mill at Bentley."

Roland burst out laughing and Jason had to wait until his friend caught his breath.

"Honey, everything you do is grist for the mill. You're insanely rich, unfairly handsome, and incredibly down-to-earth. Of course we're going to gossip about you. We're also going to talk about what a bitch the guy you end up with is, simply because we'll be jealous that it wasn't one of us you took to your bed."

Jason blushed, even though he'd heard all of that before. No matter how often he heard it, it was strange, because when he looked at himself in the mirror, he saw an average-looking guy. There wasn't anything to make him stand out in a crowd.

"I don't mix business with pleasure," he mumbled.

"But it sounds like you might be," Roland pointed out. "If this Ryan is going to be helping you find out more about the monastery."

"Can we talk about something else?"

"Sure." Roland paused and the tapping began again. "Would you like to know how much money you'll be losing if you can't finish the monastery and get it opened for business?"

"No thanks," Jason answered dryly.

"Well then you're going to have to shut down the rumours that the place is haunted."

"I don't know, Roland. I've been thinking maybe a haunted resort might bring in even more guests." Of course Jason wasn't serious, but he knew it would throw Roland off track.

"Gay men don't do haunted. You should know that by now."

"Yeah, well then you'd better use your charm to find out everything you can from that librarian, because until I know exactly what I'm up against, I'm screwed."

A noise drew his attention. Jason turned and spotted Ryan coming down the hall.

"Roland, thanks for the update. Do some more digging for me, and I'll talk to you tomorrow."

"Sure thing, boss. Don't get too caught up in work. Have some fun corrupting that almost priest of yours."

"Good-bye, bitch." Jason punched the end button and angled his body even more to meet Ryan's gaze. "Sleep well?"

"Yes, I'm sorry for passing out on you like that." Ryan ran his hand through his hair. "Guess I was more tired than I thought."

"No big deal. I got some work done, checked in with my assistant at headquarters." Jason pushed to his feet and strolled over to the other man. He reached out and trailed his finger over Ryan's cheek. "You look less stressed."

"I feel better." Ryan wandered over to the chair and sat. "Are you ready to go and look through the monastery?"

Jason glanced at his watch. "The workers should have packed up for the day. I'm ready to go over, but I get the feeling this is going to be harder on you than me, so the question is, are *you* ready?"

Ryan nodded, but Jason could sense his reluctance.

"We don't have to do it today. We can wait. Whatever's in there will still be there tomorrow."

Jason saw Ryan straighten his shoulders and climb to his feet.

"No. We'll do it now. Running away isn't the best way to face our fears."

"It's worked for me so far," Jason muttered as they headed towards the front door.

Chapter Six

Ryan shot Jason a small smile as they left the cottage, letting him know the deacon had heard his last comment. Jason gestured for Ryan to follow him as he led the way up the path towards the monastery. He tried not to think about the man and how good Ryan looked, all sleep rumpled and relaxed.

Yet the closer they got to the building, the more tension filled the air. Jason slowed his pace to let Ryan walk beside him. They stopped at the bottom of the steps leading up to the front door. Turning, Jason focused on Ryan.

The younger man's hands were clenched into fists. He stared up at the facade of the monastery as if he were facing his doom. If Ryan had been a dog, all his fur would have been standing up. Jason reached out and gripped Ryan's arms, forcing him to meet his gaze.

"We don't have to do this right now, Ryan." Jason winked, trying to relieve some of the stress. "We could go back to my place and find something much more interesting to do."

Ryan blushed, but didn't drop his gaze. "No. We have to do this, Jason. I believe the situation's only going to get worse if we don't do something."

"But I get the feeling whatever spirit is in there doesn't want us there." Jason took one of Ryan's hands in his as he whirled around to face the monastery again.

"You're half right," Ryan agreed.

"Half right? Which half would that be?" He sent Ryan a puzzled glance.

"The part where there is a spirit that doesn't want us in there, but there's also a spirit, or more than one, that wants us to come in. I can feel it tugging on me."

"Tugging on you? You can physically feel the spirits touching you, even while we're standing out here? I thought they wouldn't affect you until we went inside." Jason shivered, not liking the sound of Ryan's experiences.

Ryan tilted his head, listening to something beyond Jason's ability to hear or feel. He held tightly to Ryan's hand and frowned as the man's flesh turned cold.

"He needs our help," Ryan finally said. He turned to stare at Jason. Although Ryan held Jason's gaze, he seemed to be listening to something else. After several seconds, Ryan blinked. "We have to find him."

"Who?"

Shaking his head, Ryan returned from wherever he'd gone in his mind. "I don't know."

Jason didn't believe Ryan, but being an adult, Ryan had the right to lie to Jason about things. Not that Jason wanted him to lie. He trudged up the stairs, reluctant to enter the building. Bad things were going to happen, and

Jason didn't know how he was going to stop them. It felt like Ryan risked a lot to help him out.

He tugged on the door handle and frowned when nothing happened. "What the hell? Hank wouldn't have locked it since he knew I was going to be coming in later."

After wrapping both his hands around the handle, he yanked on it with the same results. The door didn't budge. He looked over at Ryan.

"We've never had trouble with these doors before, but I guess the constant use probably caused them to swell or something. Let's go around to the garden side. There are doors leading into some of the rooms on the first floor."

Ryan stayed silent as they made their way to the left side of the monastery. Jason entwined his fingers with Ryan's, keeping him close. Every instinct Jason had told him not to let Ryan out of his sight and he didn't plan to do so. He didn't understand why his attraction to the man had morphed into protectiveness. Jason rarely felt anything but lust for his sexual encounters, definitely never any sort of permanent emotions. Yet something about Ryan made Jason want to wrap him in a tight embrace and never let him go.

They came to a set of French doors leading into what had once been a study. Jason turned the knob and nothing happened. As he tugged on it, the oddest sensation of cold crept over his fingers and crawled up his arm. *Shit*. It was like frostbite travelling across his skin, freezing each inch it touched. Gritting his teeth, he jerked his hand away from the door and shook it.

"What the fuck is going on? None of these doors should be locked," he muttered. "I'll have to go get my keys. Hank shouldn't have locked them. He knows I check the place out after everyone leaves."

"No."

Jason turned to look at Ryan. The deacon stood, staring up at the fourth floor windows. Ryan's pale face held apprehension and resignation. Whatever was going on with the stupid doors, Ryan had an idea but wasn't sharing. After moving to the steps heading down into the garden, Jason glanced over his shoulder into the study.

A shadow stood there, blocking his view. He gasped and stopped, whirling around to stare directly at the spirit. It wasn't a trick of the light or a shadow cast by something. Jason knew the study was empty because they had taken out the shelves and books earlier in the week. Yet something was there, and the hair at the back of his neck stood up as rage hit him like a solid blow. He stumbled slightly and Ryan grabbed his arm.

"What's wrong?"

Jason waved a weak hand towards the room. "Don't you see it?"

But when they both looked back, the vision had gone. Jason shook his head. "Now they're just messing with us."

"I don't think it's you they're messing with, actually. I think they're reacting to my presence."

"Is that why we can't get in there? I thought you said they wanted your help." He straightened and slipped his arm around Ryan's shoulders. "I think we need to retreat and regroup."

"Sounds good to me," Ryan agreed. "I'm not sure about which spirits reside in the monastery. It's a little confusing, simply because I haven't been inside and in direct contact with them."

"Hmmm...well, it looks like direct contact will have to wait until later." Jason decided a course of action in his mind. "Come on. We'll have dinner and talk about this a little more. Maybe I should get a professional ghost hunting team in here or something. I've seen them on TV, though they probably wouldn't be able to get rid of the ghosts for me."

Ryan shook his head. "Some of them have people they call on to remove the spirits, but most of them are just out to document that spirits exist. I think you want your spirits gone. Not good business practice to have the guests frightened."

Jason shrugged. "I could always market it as a haunted resort. There are people who would pay a lot of money to spend the night in a ghost-ridden building."

"The idea of it being haunted is fun, but the first time they actually come into contact with one of the spirits, they'd run for the hills."

"True. I think we're better off getting rid of them altogether and making this place a five-star resort for gay men." He winked at Ryan.

The younger man chuckled and encircled Jason's waist with his arm. "It's an ambitious plan, but I get the feeling you get what you want when you put your mind to it."

"Haven't been denied yet." Jason nuzzled Ryan's auburn hair.

Ryan tensed slightly and Jason started to move away, but the tight grip on his waist kept him from straying too far.

"No, don't." Ryan sounded frustrated. "I'm not used to touching and being close to another man like this."

"Well, if we continue to work together on this spirit problem, you'll have to get used to it. I'm a touchy-feely kind of guy, especially when I like someone." He leant down and brushed his lips over Ryan's cheek. "And I happen to really like you."

Ryan squeaked softly and Jason thought it was adorable, but he didn't push any further. He wanted Ryan relaxed and willing, not nervous or freaked out. He was pretty sure they'd end up in bed together, but not until Ryan said it was okay. Forcing a guy wasn't Jason's style.

"What would you like for dinner? We can either make something or order take-out. I'm easy either way."

The soft laugh coming from Ryan told Jason the gentle man understood the innuendo. Jason's laughter burst out of him and he urged Ryan down the walk towards the cottage.

"So you know my deep dark secret. I'm easy about pretty much everything, unless it's work. Then I can be a hard-nosed bastard." He lifted a shoulder. "I guess it comes from my dad. He died when I was fifteen, but he proved to me that with hard work, you can do anything. With where we lived, Dad became a miner like almost every other boy in the town, but he didn't want that for me. Taught me if something was going to have my name on it, it better be the best thing I could build."

Ryan nodded, but didn't speak about his own family. Jason didn't pry either. The reaction Ryan had had earlier in the day while discussing his past told Jason the slender man had more issues than just trying to decide if he wanted to be a priest or not.

"What do you have to make for dinner?" Ryan peeked at him through his lashes. "I'm not interested in going out."

There were so many ways to interpret those words, and Jason didn't want to assume the wrong thing. He thought about what he had in his refrigerator and cupboards.

"I have spaghetti and the makings for home-made sauce, plus we can make garlic bread. I have lettuce for a salad."

"Do you have anything for dessert?"

He leered at Ryan. "I don't know. Do I?"

The sexy blush colouring Ryan's cheeks urged Jason to kiss the man again. He slid his hands into Ryan's hair, holding him still as he lowered his head to bring their lips together. Ryan didn't move, but his gasp allowed Jason to sweep his tongue inside.

He stroked along Ryan's teeth and tongue, enjoying the little whimpers Ryan made as Jason's hands roamed down to cup Ryan's ass. Rocking their groins together, Jason dragged his lips from Ryan's and trailed kisses along the man's jaw to the sensitive spot right behind his ear. He applied a little suction and Ryan jerked like an electric shock had rippled through him.

"Oh," Ryan breathed, encircling Jason's shoulders with his arms before he went limp in Jason's embrace.

"You like that, don't you?" Jason nibbled along the outside of Ryan's ear.

Ryan's trembling body told Jason all the things Ryan couldn't. Jason eased his hand around and pressed it to the bulge in Ryan's pants. Ryan closed his eyes and ground his erection into Jason's palm. Keeping his touch firm, but not backing off or strengthening his grip, Jason sucked on Ryan's earlobe.

"I haven't...ever," Ryan stammered.

"Haven't what? Come in your pants? Had someone help you come?"

Jason eased back a little to meet Ryan's embarrassed gaze. Oh, he didn't like that look at all. Ryan should never be ashamed about his lack of experience. Hell, it turned Jason on to know that no one had ever touched Ryan like he was at the moment.

"How about all of the above," Ryan whispered.

"You don't know what a turn-on that is," Jason admitted, but he stepped away.

Ryan's moan of protest brought a smile to Jason's face.

"Don't worry, honey. I'll make sure you come, but not in your pants or out here." He waved a hand to include the garden they stood in. "When you come, I want you naked in my bed, so I can hold you afterwards."

"Okay."

There wasn't any hesitation in Ryan's agreement, yet Jason knew the instant the need wore off, Ryan would start thinking about the consequences and ramifications of their actions. Jason wasn't sure how he felt about that, but he knew he had to let Ryan come to the decision on his own, without pressure.

"Let's go cook dinner before we worry about dessert."

Ryan looked puzzled by Jason's retreat, but he smiled when Jason held out his hand. They strolled in the direction of the caretaker's cottage. Ryan suddenly stopped. When Jason looked back to see what was wrong, Ryan's eyes were closed, his head tilted to the side. Jason had a feeling Ryan was once again listening to ghostly voices only he could hear.

"Ryan?" he prompted.

Ryan's eyelids opened. "Sorry."

"Don't be." Jason wrapped a comforting arm around Ryan's waist. "Have you changed your mind about dinner?"

Ryan shook his head. Although he appeared troubled, he gestured towards the cottage. "Talk to me about something else. I need to get these voices out of my head for a while."

Jason nodded. "I can do that."

The light conversation continued through dinner. Jason didn't back off from touching Ryan; on the hip, the back or brushing their hands together as they reached for something at the same time. In many ways, it was a slow seduction. He wanted Ryan to get used to Jason being in his personal space.

After the dishes were cleaned and put away, Jason took Ryan's hand and led him into the living room.

"Let me give you a tour of the cottage."

"I've already seen most of it." Ryan shot him an amused glance. "Is this tour going to end up in your bedroom?"

Jason ducked his head, and if his laugh sounded a little hesitant, he didn't think Ryan would blame him.

"I was hoping it would," he confessed, looking back up to meet Ryan's gaze.

"Well, let's just go there straight away." When Jason didn't move, Ryan pushed him slightly. "What are you waiting for?"

"I guess I'm still a little unsure that you can change your mind so quickly. I mean one minute you're going to be a priest. The next, you're gay and ready for me to fuck you."

"Who said anything about you taking me?" Ryan's eyes glinted as he teased. "Maybe I want to take you."

Hearing those words coming from that innocent face stiffened Jason's cock even more.

"It doesn't matter who gets fucked. I just want to make sure you're not going to regret it in the morning." Jason shoved his hand through his hair. "Listen, I'm used to being someone's mistake, but I'm not used to being someone's first. It would really suck if we slept together, and then tomorrow when we woke up, you're hit with guilt and run back to the church." He sighed and paced the hallway. "Seducing a priest might be some people's secret fantasy, but it's never been mine."

Whatever doubt or worry Ryan had earlier seemed gone as the man grabbed Jason by the hand and dragged him down to the bedroom. They stepped inside and Ryan shut the door. He turned and cradled Jason's face in his hands. His earnest dark green eyes met Jason's, and Jason fell into them without fear.

"I can't promise I won't freak out in the morning. Most of my life, I've planned for the day I'd become a priest. The church provided me protection when I needed it the most, but I think deep inside, I've always known this moment would come."

Ryan's crooked smile tugged at Jason's heart. "The closer I got to my ordination, the more I thought about what I really wanted out of life. I don't want to live in guilt or fear that my sexual orientation will be found out. If I decide to become a priest, I'm choosing to deny a very real part of myself. I can't do that and be happy. There are just some things prayer can't fix."

"Fix? You say that as though you're broken. I believe I was made this way. You're the one who believes so strongly in God. Do you think he would make an entire section of the population this way by mistake?" Jason shook his head. "I refuse to believe that."

Ryan nodded. "You're right. Even though I've felt the same way, it helps to hear someone else say it. I believe God wants all his children to live a life of love and happiness. If this is the path that makes me happy, I'm sure God wouldn't love me any less for it."

The confidence and conviction shining in Ryan's eyes broke down Jason's last walls of doubt. They would deal with Ryan's reaction tomorrow. Tonight was for introducing Ryan to all the joys of sex and hopefully it'd be good enough for Ryan to want to do it as often as possible.

"Good. Then we agree." Jason reached out and started unbuttoning Ryan's shirt. As each inch of flesh appeared, Jason pressed an open-mouthed kiss to it. Ryan gasped and his hands landed on Jason's hips, fingers flexing with each caress.

Stepping back a few inches, Jason stripped off his shirt. "You can touch me too, Ryan. I don't mind."

"I'm not sure what to do. I don't want to bother you." Ryan ducked his head.

Jason placed his knuckle under Ryan's chin and lifted it. He waited until Ryan met his gaze. "If you bother me, it'll only be in a good way. If you enjoy how I touch you, then I imagine I'd enjoy it as well. You can do that until you feel more confident about going out on your own. I won't tell you no."

"That's good to know, even though it might take me a little while to get used to being naked with another man."

Ryan ran his hands over Jason's chest, pinching his nipples and drawing a moan from him. He shoved Ryan's shirt off and wrapped his arms around the man's waist. Their bodies went together like Ryan had been carved to fit against Jason perfectly.

Bending, he wrapped his lips around Ryan's nipple and flicked it with his tongue. Ryan jerked and Jason chuckled, but did it again.

"Oh wow," Ryan's voice was breathy.

"It's like your nipple's directly attached to your cock, isn't it?"

"Yeah."

He teased and played with Ryan's nipples while Ryan ran his hands all over Jason's back. Ryan's soft groans and moans clued Jason in on when he should move on. He slipped to his knees and undid Ryan's pants.

"Jason?"

Looking up, he met Ryan's gaze. "Yes?"

"I think I need to sit down before you do anything else."

Jason took in Ryan's flushed skin and the slight tremble of his hands. "Okay. Let's get naked and you can sit down."

"Umm…" Ryan hesitated.

Grasping what a big event it was for Ryan, Jason paused and thought for a moment.

"Do you want me to get the rubbers from the bathroom while you undress? You can climb under the covers if you want before I get back."

"Thank you."

He trailed his fingers over Ryan's cheek. "No problem. I know how embarrassing all this can be. It may have been years ago, but I still remember my first time."

Jason headed into the bathroom off the master bedroom, and rustled around the cabinet under the sink. He found the new box of condoms he'd bought, not because he thought he'd end up in bed with the deacon, but because he never knew when he might meet someone he wanted to sleep with. It paid to be prepared.

He knocked on the door before leaving the bathroom. "Are you ready?"

"Yes."

He stepped out to see Ryan in bed with the covers pulled up to his neck. Jason walked over to the bed and sat beside Ryan. Bracing his hands on either side of Ryan's head, Jason leant over and brushed a kiss over Ryan's lips.

"Are you sure you want to do this?" He rubbed a thumb over Ryan's bottom lip. "Because if you've changed your mind, I won't get angry or anything. I'm not going to push you into something you're not sure of."

"No. I'm fine. Just nervous. I don't want to disappoint you," Ryan admitted, gaze dropping to stare at Jason's chest.

"Not possible," Jason fired back with another kiss. "Can I climb in there with you?"

Nodding, Ryan held up the corner of the comforter. "Thanks for understanding."

As much as Jason wanted to jump Ryan and fuck him until he screamed, he knew it wasn't the way to go about introducing Ryan to sex. He crawled in and settled next to Ryan, propping himself up on his elbow. Ryan lay on his back, smiling up at Jason. The trust shining in Ryan's green eyes was humbling. He'd never been someone's first, and the enormous responsibility hit him.

"How about we just make out for a little while? If we feel like going further, we will."

Ryan nodded again while he reached and slid his hand around the back of Jason's head. Jason allowed him to tug him down until their lips met. The kiss was soft and slow, learning each groove in Ryan's teeth and what made him shiver. Jason caressed Ryan's body, distracting the man from everything except how he felt. Pleasure shot through him as Ryan began to touch him back.

Jason lost track of how long they kissed and touched. All he knew was desire built in him in a way he'd never felt before. At some point, he shifted and wedged his body between Ryan's legs.

"Oh." Ryan blinked as their erections rubbed against each other for the first time.

"Feels good, doesn't it?" Jason rocked his hips and almost growled at the slickness of Ryan's flesh.

The pre cum leaking from their cocks smoothed the friction and Jason sped up, wanting to get Ryan off. Once he came, Ryan would be more relaxed. Changing his mind, Jason shoved the blankets out of the way and licked a path down over Ryan's chest and stomach to where the man's dick nudged Jason's chin.

He took one swipe along the entire length of Ryan's hard-on before scrambling for a condom. Tearing open the packet, he glanced up at Ryan.

"Never take a man's word that he's clean. I know you are since you're a virgin, but if I expect you to listen to me, I have to take my own advice."

Ryan blushed, but said, "I understand."

Jason rolled the latex down and wrapped his mouth around Ryan. Inch by inch, he sucked Ryan in until his nose hit the curls at the base of Ryan's cock. He swallowed and Ryan arched off the bed. Jason gagged slightly before he gripped Ryan's hips and pinned him to the mattress.

"Oh, Jason," Ryan started to babble as Jason applied suction.

He worked the hard flesh, lightly scraping his teeth over Ryan's dick. He hated the taste of the condom, but he'd deal with it to give Ryan his first blowjob. Jason fondled Ryan's balls, and reached behind them to caress the soft patch of skin. Ryan trembled and shuddered, his voice starting out soft, but getting louder the longer Jason played with him.

Without moving away, he searched through the sheets to find the bottle of lube he kept under his pillows. A small thrill of triumph went through him as his hand snatched the lube up. He somehow managed to get it open, even with all of Ryan's movements. After squirting some slick onto his fingers, he rubbed them together to warm it up a little before he started preparing Ryan for his cock.

Ryan tensed when Jason ran his finger along his crease to graze the puckered opening. Jason hummed around Ryan's cock, not wanting to let Ryan's erection out of his mouth to reassure the man. The vibrations seemed to take Ryan's mind off Jason touching him in a place no one had ever touched before.

Getting more lube, he slathered it over Ryan's opening and pressed just the tip of his finger inside the ring of muscle. Ryan stiffened and Jason let his cock pop out of his mouth to rest his head on Ryan's thigh.

"Don't tense. Push out, sweetheart. If you can relax, it'll be easier. I know it burns, but once I get you stretched, it won't be bad."

He encouraged Ryan, who took a breath and somehow managed to relax, allowing Jason's finger to sink knuckle deep into Ryan's ass.

"Holy cow," Ryan muttered.

Jason stilled, not wanting to move until Ryan told him it was okay. As soon as Ryan's inner muscles' grip eased, Jason started thrusting his finger in and out. When he thought Ryan was ready, he slid two, then three fingers in, stretching and relaxing him.

On one push in, he nailed Ryan's gland and Ryan yelled. Jason took Ryan back into his mouth and began stoking the desire burning in Ryan.

"Jason, please," Ryan begged and Jason twisted his fingers, brushing against the hot spot every chance he could.

Ryan talked and moaned, though Jason couldn't understand anything the man said. He just focussed on driving Ryan crazy. He wanted Ryan to come before he took him. He winced when Ryan gripped his hair and tugged.

"Jason…I'm going to come," Ryan panted.

Go ahead, Jason thought but kept his mouth on Ryan. He took Ryan all the way down and swallowed while pressing against Ryan's gland.

"Jason!" Ryan shouted and his cock throbbed as he came.

Jason massaged all he could out of Ryan. Finally, he let Ryan slip out of his mouth when the man flopped back on the bed. He grabbed another condom and rolled it on his own aching erection.

Arranging Ryan's legs over his arms, he positioned his cock at Ryan's opening. He met Ryan's gaze as he sank in. Ryan's eyes widened and he bit his lip as Jason filled him. He didn't break their connection as he began to move, sliding in and out.

His climax wouldn't be long in arriving. Bringing Ryan off first had caused Jason's need to build until all Ryan had to do was clench his inner passage and Jason's climax crashed over him.

"Fuck," Jason shouted and filled the condom.

His strength drained, Jason fell forward, catching himself on his arms before he squashed Ryan. Panting, he brushed a kiss over Ryan's lips and rolled to his side. He stared up at the ceiling until his pulse slowed and he gained control of his muscles.

"Jason," Ryan started.

Jason pressed his finger to his lover's lips and shook his head. "Let me clean us up before we talk."

Ryan smiled and Jason crawled out of bed, grabbing a tissue from his nightstand to wrap Ryan's condom. He carried it to the bathroom where he tossed it in the trash along with his. He cleaned up and wet a cloth to take care of Ryan. Heading back to the bedroom, Jason grinned at how debauched Ryan looked with a satisfied expression on his face.

Jason washed Ryan up and tossed the cloth onto the floor. He slipped back under the blankets and pulled Ryan against him.

"Thank you," Ryan whispered.

"Thank you, Ryan, for letting me be your first." Jason nuzzled the nape of Ryan's neck. He knew Ryan wanted to talk, but Jason had been around long enough to know pillow talk usually led to hurt feelings and broken promises. *No.* He didn't want that with Ryan. Whatever direction their relationship took from here on, it should happen naturally. "Why don't you go to sleep? I'll make sure you get up early enough to head to the rectory if you need to."

He waited for Ryan to tense and run off, but the slender man didn't move, just wiggled back closer to Jason.

"That's fine. I could cook you breakfast before I go."

Okay. Jason mentally shrugged. There would probably be regret and guilt in the morning, but he'd take Ryan's presence in his bed and arms for now. He kissed Ryan's shoulder again and closed his eyes. Sleep caught him unawares and he dozed off quickly, holding Ryan tight.

Chapter Seven

Ryan gasped at the sight of Bishop Adler's car in the driveway. "Oh no."

Jason pulled his car alongside the kerb and put it in park. "Do you want me to come in with you?"

"No!" Ryan shouted before he could stop himself. "Sorry." He reached out and squeezed Jason's hand. "I didn't mean to yell at you. It's just something I'm going to have to face on my own."

"Whose car is it?" Jason asked.

"Bishop Adler's." Ryan shook his head and looked at the house. "Of all the people to catch me staying out all night…"

"You could tell him you were giving comfort to someone in need," Jason suggested.

"I can't lie to him."

"You wouldn't be."

Ryan's breath caught. Did Jason really need him or did he simply need someone? What would it be like to have someone feel such a base emotion for him? "I should go."

Jason rubbed Ryan's knuckles. "Call or come by as soon as you can. Until I hear from you, I'll worry."

"I will." Ryan pulled his hand away and opened the car door. "Who knows, maybe I'll get lucky and Bishop Adler will give me some answers about St. Xavier before he tosses me out of the church on my ass."

"If he does, and you need a place to stay, you know where to find me."

Ryan shook his head. Although the idea of taking refuge with Jason was appealing, Ryan knew it wouldn't be right. One night of unforgettable passion didn't equate to shacking up. "I'll figure something out," he mumbled before getting out of the car.

He smiled once more at Jason before shutting the door and making his way towards the rectory. Ryan had known he'd have to talk to his spiritual mentor, but he'd hoped he'd have more time to figure out what to say. *Well, time's up,* he said to himself as he walked into the house.

"Where have you been?" Bishop Adler asked from his position on the sofa.

"St. Xavier," Ryan replied. He stood just inside the door with his hands clasped behind his back.

"I told you to forget about the monastery."

"Yes, you did, but the owner came to me for help, and I couldn't turn him away." Ryan crossed to one of the wingback chairs and sat uneasily. "There are spirits trapped there."

Bishop Adler's facial expression didn't change at the announcement. "You knew," Ryan surmised.

"Leave it," Joseph replied.

"I can't do that." Ryan leant forward in the chair. "How can you?"

"Because I was there that day, and I saw what she did to them. Believe me, son, no amount of prayer is going to rid that place of the tragedy that unfolded there."

"How do you know? Have you tried?" Ryan asked.

"No, and I never will. Stirring them up will only make things worse for them and for the Church."

"Why? Tell me what really happened that day." Ryan held his breath. Maybe he'd finally get some answers to the whispered words that sang in his ears every time he stepped foot outside Jason's cottage.

"Just as soon as you tell me why you've been out all night."

Was the bishop playing a game of tit for tat? Ryan had no doubt there would be absolutely no tat coming his way after he informed Bishop Adler that he'd spent the night with Jason Bentley. "I've already told you where I was."

Joseph's eyes narrowed. "Why do I find it difficult to believe you spent the night in the monastery?" The sneer on his face as he asked the question told Ryan he already knew the answer.

"Actually, I spent the night in the caretaker's cottage." Before the bishop could respond, Ryan continued. "You've done so much for me over the years, and it's with deep regret that I tell you this, but I've decided to resign from my position with the church."

Joseph exploded out of his seat. He stalked towards Ryan with fisted hands at his side. "After all I've done, you've given yourself over to the evil that lurks inside of you!"

Ryan held his ground. "There's no evil inside me. I've prayed to God for years for an answer, and I truly believe he's given me one. I'm sorry that I've hurt you, but I can't deny who I am any longer. The Church will always be a big part of my life, but I feel I'm meant to do something else with it."

"The church doesn't condone homosexuality. You'll no longer be welcomed within the sacred nave."

Ryan shook his head. "The Catholic Church may not believe I'm worthy, but God does and always will. There are other churches out there. My faith is stronger than your misbegotten beliefs."

"Please don't give yourself over to the evil that flows through your veins. Is the lure of the flesh so important to you that you would condemn yourself to such a fate?"

Ryan chose to ignore Bishop Adler's condemnation. The decision had been made and nothing the man spewed would change that. "I'll be out before nightfall."

"You'll be out this minute," Joseph countered. "I've done everything for you, and if you choose to turn your back on the church, you'll leave here empty-handed. You have absolutely nothing the church didn't pay for."

"You're wrong about that." Ryan started in the direction of the staircase leading to his room. When the bishop began to charge after him, Ryan picked up his pace, taking the steps two at a time.

Entering his room, he shut and locked the door before the older man could make it up the stairs. He retrieved his Bible from his bedside table and the shabby-looking teddy bear along with a small overnight bag from the top shelf of his closet.

"Open this door," Joseph bellowed.

Ryan hurried to the dresser and opened his bottom drawer. He pulled out the jeans and T-shirts from his high school days and shoved them into the duffle. Ryan stood and opened his sock and underwear drawer. He started to add those to his bag but stopped himself. "No," he said aloud to the newer items of clothing.

He placed his Bible carefully in the duffle and tucked his teddy bear under his arm. Opening the door, he came face to face with Bishop Adler. "I took only what was mine before I came to live here."

Ryan was surprised to find tears filling the bishop's eyes. "I'm sorry it has to end this way."

When Bishop Adler said nothing, Ryan went around the older man and down the stairs. Before he reached the front door, he heard the bishop call out to him. Ryan stopped and looked up at the landing at the top of the steps.

"Don't go back to the monastery. I beg you. Nothing good can, or will, come from it."

Before Ryan could question him further, Bishop Adler turned and walked back down the hall. Ryan briefly wondered if the bishop was going back to Father Paul's room to ransack it some more. In the end, he knew it didn't matter. He no longer belonged to the bishop's world. He turned and walked out, his meagre belongings in hand.

* * * *

On his way to the monastery, Ryan stopped by the Catholic cemetery. Although he could search the area on his own, he decided to take a chance and knocked on the groundskeeper's door.

When he received no reply, Ryan took a deep breath and started for the front of the cemetery. As he moved down the rows, he scanned the dates on the headstones.

"May I help you?" a voice said from behind him.

Ryan turned to find the groundskeeper. "Hi, Abe."

"Deacon Christopher? What're you doing wandering the cemetery?" the old man asked.

"I've been trying to find out some of the history surrounding the murders at St. Xavier. I guess I hoped I'd find something here."

Abe took off his ball cap and rubbed his aging scalp. "Why would you be doing that?"

"Just a project I'm working on. Can you tell me if the nuns from St. Xavier are buried here?"

"Yeah." Abe pointed towards the east side of the grounds. They're all over there except the one."

Ryan searched his memory trying to come up with the name Bishop Adler had supplied. "Sister Cawfield?"

"That her name?" Abe asked, resettling his hat. "Can't say I recall that name, but yeah, I remember something about her being buried over in the Holy Springs Cemetery across town."

"And the priest that died, Father Clennan? Is he here?"

A shadow seemed to pass over Abe's expression. With a curt nod, he started walking. "Follow me."

Ryan wondered about Abe's change in attitude. Although he didn't know the man well, he'd dealt with him in a professional capacity on several occasions, most recently at Father Paul's funeral.

When he noticed Abe veering off to the left instead of heading towards the section Father Paul was buried in, he stopped. "He's not with the other clergy?"

Abe shook his head and kept walking. He eventually stopped beside a small headstone and pointed downwards. "This is it."

Father Clennan's final resting place may have only been forty yards or so from the other deceased priests, but the gravesite was vastly different in appearance. Not only was Father Clennan's headstone much smaller, but there were no flowers or urns to decorate the grave.

Ryan looked in the direction of Father Paul's grave. Bright red and purple silk flowers filled the urns on either side of not only Paul's headstone, but all of the priests' graves. "Why's Father Clennan all the way over here?"

"Don't know," Abe replied. "I'd imagine it has something to do with how and where he died, but the church don't tell me that stuff."

"Thanks." Ryan took a mental note of the day of Father Clennan's death to help him in his search for the truth of what had happened that day. He gave the old man a gentle pat on the shoulder before walking off towards where the nuns were buried.

There were nine gravestones with the exact same date on them. Ryan's head popped up and scanned the cemetery, spotting Abe disappearing into a shed. He took off at a run back to the man he hoped would have some answers. "Hey, Abe?"

After a few moments of the sound of clattering equipment, Abe stuck his head out of the shed door. "Somethin' else you need, Deacon?"

"Yeah. I noticed the nuns' day of death is one day earlier than Father Clennan's. Can you tell me why that is?"

"Guess I never noticed that. I do remember that they were all buried the same day though because it liked to kill me trying to get that many graves dug in time. I had to call in three of my brothers to help me."

"Thanks." Ryan started to walk back towards the front gate.

"You might check the county death records," Abe suggested.

112

"Good idea. Thanks." With that plan in mind, Ryan went back to the nuns' graves and wrote down each of their names. He wondered if Jason would be able to access the records online.

Armed with his list, Ryan picked up his meagre belongings and took off towards St. Xavier.

* * * *

Before he reached the monastery, Ryan realised he had no choice but to ask Jason for a place to stay until he could...what? He sat at the corner of the St. Xavier property and leant back against the iron fence. Ryan buried his face in his hands and did his best not to break down. Twenty-five years old and starting from scratch. What would he do with his life now?

He liked Jason, a lot, but he didn't want to be the kind of man who latched onto someone because he had no one else. Ryan groaned. Even though he really, really wanted to be with Jason again, he knew he'd worry that Jason would see him as desperate.

"One of my workers told me I had a vagrant out here," Jason said from behind Ryan.

Ryan looked over his shoulder before glancing down at his duffle bag. "He'd be right."

Jason sat down on the opposite side of the fence. "What happened?"

"What didn't?" Ryan gestured to his belongings before turning around to face Jason. "Within the span of an hour, I gave up my career, got thrown out of my home and probably lost the only man who ever really loved me."

Carol Lynne & T.A. Chase

Jason reached through the iron bars to cup Ryan's cheek. "Either that man never really loved you or you haven't really lost him."

Ryan closed his eyes and tried to soak up Jason's strength and kindness. If only he could believe that he would still have his mentor, but he doubted he'd ever speak to Bishop Adler again. The real kicker was that it hurt more than he'd ever admit. Relinquishing his spot in the church wasn't easy, but he still had God in his life. Giving up Joseph Adler would be giving up the only person he thought of as family.

Bringing Jason's mood down wasn't what Ryan wanted though. "I went by the cemetery on my way here."

Jason's brows drew together in obvious confusion. "Is that a good thing?"

Ryan shrugged and pulled the slip of paper from his pocket. "Do you know how to look up death records on the internet?"

"Umm, well, I can't say that I've ever done it before, but I'm sure willing to give it a shot. What're you looking for?"

Ryan handed the paper through the fence. "The date of death on the nuns' headstones doesn't match the one on Father Clennan's. I thought maybe we could find out why."

"I already know why. Roland, my assistant, called earlier. He sweet talked an old librarian here in town."

When Jason didn't continue, Ryan threw up his hands in exasperation. "Well? What did she tell him?"

Jason grinned. "Come over on this side, and I'll tell ya."

Chuckling, Ryan got to his feet. He shoved his duffle and teddy bear through the fence. "Hold that." As he ran to the gate, he couldn't wipe the smile from his face. By

114

the time he'd rounded the fence and reached Jason, he launched himself at the man who had the ability to make him feel good even on the worst day of his life.

"Oompfff." Jason fell backwards onto the soft grass with Ryan wrapped in his arms. "What was that for?" he asked, staring up at Ryan.

"For making me smile," Ryan said before pulling Jason's head down for a kiss.

Ryan moaned when he felt the brush of Jason's tongue against his. Kissing was definitely better than candy. He rolled to the side, pulling Jason on top of him. The feel of Jason's bigger body pressing down on all the right spots kicked Ryan's lust into overdrive. He wrapped his legs around Jason's hips and squirmed with the delicious rub to his hard cock.

"Jason!" someone shouted.

Jason broke the kiss and groaned. "Yeah, Hank?"

Hank came to stand over them, an embarrassed flush to his face. "Oh, sorry. The guys told me you came out to deal with someone hanging around outside the gate. When I saw you on the ground…well, I came to help, but it's obvious you have everything under control."

Jason answered Hank but continued to stare down at Ryan. "Yeah, I've got everything well in hand."

Ryan glanced up at Hank. He was mortified to be found in such a position, but Jason obviously wasn't bothered. "Hank," he acknowledged.

"Deacon," Hank greeted in return.

"Just Ryan now," he said, feeling the need to set the man straight. He shifted his attention to Jason when the man started to move his hips. Ryan narrowed his eyes at the man trying to make him come despite the fact they were being watched.

Jason chuckled and did it again. "You can take off, Hank."

"Yeah...uh...I need to make a phone call," Hank stammered before turning to jog back to the monastery.

"What're you doing?" Ryan asked.

"Rubbing my cock against you. Why, you gonna tell me you don't like it?"

Ryan hitched his legs higher around Jason's waist. "What I like and what's appropriate ten feet from the road are two different things."

"When I want something, I've never been good at depriving myself. No matter who's around. Besides, people driving by can't see us nearly as well as the guys up on the third and fourth floors can." Jason pushed one hand between them and ran his fingertip over the length of Ryan's zipper. "Does that bother you?"

Ryan thought about it for several moments while Jason slowly lowered the zipper on Ryan's pants. It wasn't until Jason pulled Ryan's cock free that the answer came to him. "It doesn't bother me that people can see us kissing and stuff, but I don't think I'm quite ready to flash my cock to the world."

With a chuckle, Jason gave Ryan's erection one more squeeze before tucking it back into his pants. "Fair enough." Jason sat back on his heels, and Ryan quickly zipped himself up. "We'll have to work on that though." Jason winked and stood, holding out his hand.

Ryan wasted no time in taking the offered gesture. He stood and once again pressed himself against Jason's body. He honestly didn't see himself ever being able to perform in front of other people. With the line of work Jason was in, Ryan began to worry. "Is that a requirement to be with you?"

"Requirement? No. But I'm hoping you'll stick around for a while and sooner or later, you're going to see others doing what we almost did." Jason gestured to the monastery. "This will be a place for couples to indulge in their fantasies. A week-long refuge where men can come without worry of disapproving looks if they want to touch each other. It's giving them that freedom that's made The Bentley Corporation what it is."

Ryan buried his face against Jason's neck. He couldn't believe the man actually wanted him to stick around. They'd only known each other a short time. Was Jason feeling the same thing Ryan felt? He assumed his overpowering need to be with the man had more to do with his inexperience, but Jason was far from a shy virgin.

"It might take time for me to get used to seeing what I've only seen on the internet so far, but I'll try."

"That's all I can ask." Jason started off towards the building, his arm wrapped around Ryan's waist.

The sight of the nun in the fourth floor window made Ryan shiver. It reminded him of the danger that still lay ahead.

"You okay?" Jason asked, kissing the top of Ryan's head.

Ryan nodded. "I was hoping to be fully prepared before entering the monastery, but the more digging I do, the more questions I have."

"Well, like I told you before, Roland gave me some new information. Maybe that'll help?"

"Maybe, but I have a strong feeling I won't get the answers I need until I suck it up and try to talk to Sister Ann Cawfield. She seems to be the one trying the hardest to get my attention."

* * * *

"Wait a minute. You're telling me the nuns were dead a full day before Father Clennan was killed?" Ryan asked. He sat up in bed, letting the covers pool around his groin.

"According to the librarian, that was the coroner's finding. Of course that was a long time ago. I'm sure they couldn't pinpoint the exact time of death like they can now."

Ryan crawled out of bed and walked to the window that overlooked the monastery. The sun was starting to fade as, one by one, the workers began leaving for the day. Bracing his hands on either side of the glass, Ryan stared at the fourth floor. "What about Sister Cawfield? Did the librarian say anything about her?"

Jason's warm body pressed against Ryan from behind. "She told Roland that from what she heard at the time, Sister Cawfield was a bloody mess when they removed her body." He kissed Ryan's neck. "You're giving Hank quite a show, you know?"

"Huh?" Ryan absently asked, tilting his head to the side.

Jason licked a path up Ryan's neck to his ear. "Bottom floor, second window."

Ryan's gaze followed the directions. Hank was looking straight at him. It wasn't until that moment Ryan remembered he was completely naked, practically pressed against the window.

Ryan started to take a step back when he froze in his tracks. A dark figure appeared just behind Hank. It only took Ryan a moment to realise who the figure was. "Why would Father Clennan's spirit still be in the monastery?"

"What?"

"There, behind Hank." When Ryan gestured towards the window where Hank was, Hank must've known he'd been caught looking. Hank's eyes rounded, but before he could step back, he was suddenly airborne, being pushed through the large pane of glass.

"Call 9-1-1," Jason said, grabbing his jeans before running from the room.

* * * *

While paramedics worked to stabilise Hank, Jason spoke with the police, his hands and bare chest still covered in Hank's drying blood. Ryan watched his lover try to explain the unexplainable.

Ryan turned his attention to the building. *Enough!* What if it had been Jason who'd been shoved through the window? He stormed towards the monastery and was shocked when the door opened for him on the first try. Easing the door shut, Ryan engaged the lock. He knew it wouldn't be enough to keep Jason out, but it was all he could do to warn his lover not to follow him.

Opening himself to the spirits around him, Ryan slowly walked towards the library Hank had used for his office. He didn't dare enter the room out of fear of being spotted by Jason or the police. In the end, it didn't matter. Father Clennan's ghost wasn't in the room.

Ryan turned and made his way back to the entrance. With his hand on the heavily carved banister, he started up the steps. "I'm here. Talk to me."

He was halfway up the staircase when he felt the push. The unexpected assault threw him off balance. He rolled head over heels to the bottom, smacking his face against one of the banisters on his way down.

With a groan, Ryan sat up and felt the blood run into his eyes. He reached up and felt the gash on his forehead. "If you don't want me here, why do you keep showing yourself to me?"

Ryan pulled his T-shirt off and wrapped it around his head. "You'll have to do better than that to get rid of me." He knew he was taunting the dark spirits that roamed the building, but what did he have to lose? If he couldn't find a way to help the ghosts move on, Jason would be forced to abandon the project altogether. Even though it had been such a short time, Ryan knew if Jason left town it would kill him.

Getting to his feet, Ryan started up the staircase once again. Learning his lesson, he held tightly to the banister as he ascended the steps. He reached the second floor successfully and felt a slight stir in the air. As the atmosphere around him began to cool, Ryan made his way to the first room. Before he could cross the threshold, the images began. *Blood. Throats slashed. Eyes removed.*

It was too much at once and Ryan fell to his knees, emptying the contents of his stomach on Jason's newly refinished floor. The door slammed, striking him on the side of the head. As Ryan's world went dark, he wondered if his faith and natural abilities would ever be enough to rid the house of the pain that had occurred within its walls.

Chapter Eight

As the ambulance drove away, Jason took a deep breath and stared down at his blood stained hands. Seeing Hank being launched through the window like a ragdoll had shaken Jason to his core. Even though the bloody nun had attacked him earlier in the week, he still hadn't believed spirits could physically harm him. Not like what happened to Hank.

Shit! Without Hank to supervise, Jason was going to have to close down the construction until he could get someone else as experienced to take over. He started to scrub his face, but stopped before he smeared any more blood on his skin. He turned to look at the shards of glass all over the ground under the window. Of course, he should just close down construction until he and Ryan figured out how to put the spirits to rest.

The sound of shoes over stone brought his attention back to Officer Osmond, who stood next to him, staring at the broken window as well. Jason wasn't sure if the man believed Jason's explanation of Hank being on a ladder and falling through the window when the equipment slid on the wooden floor. There really wasn't any way to explain that the spirit of a dead priest had heaved Hank through the glass in a fit of rage or whatever the dead spirit was feeling at that moment.

"Are you shutting down the construction site?"

Jason nodded. "It'll take me a little while to get a foreman down here, and there are some issues I need to work out before I let anyone else back in."

"Like trying to figure out how to convince the guys this place isn't haunted?"

Swinging around, Jason met Osmond's gaze. "Haunted? What gives you that idea? This was just an accident."

Osmond folded his arms over his ample stomach. "Second accident on this site. Listen, I'm not a believer by any means, but something about this place puts me on edge. Now, I'm not going to run around spreading rumours or anything like that. I'm glad to see Deacon Christopher here though. If anyone can help you sort out your problems, he can."

"Thanks for keeping quiet about things for now. We're doing our best to straighten things out." Jason frowned, looking around him. "Speaking of Ryan, where is he?"

The policeman shrugged. "I don't know. He wandered off while we were talking to the paramedics. I have to head back to the station. Do you need help boarding up that window?"

"No. Ryan can help me. I'd shake your hand, Officer..." He held up his hands.

"It's okay. Go wash off and get that taken care of. It looks like rain tonight."

Fuck! Jason waved as he jogged up the front steps. He'd rinse off in the back kitchen before going to look for Ryan. As he reached for the door handle, he thought about how jinxed this entire project had been from the start. All of the workers thought the place was haunted, and now with Hank's accident, they would take it more to heart than ever.

His arm almost popped out of its socket when he yanked on the handle and the door didn't budge.

"Not fucking again," he snarled, tugging on it while fighting the urge to kick the shit out of the damned thing. He slammed his fist against the dark wood. "I don't know who the hell you are, but you need to open this fucking door. I'm not in the mood to be messed with. I'll take a fucking axe to it if you don't open it up."

Thank God everyone had left. He could just imagine how he looked, blood covered and half naked, pounding on the door while yelling at non-existent people.

"Ryan, are you in there?" Jason pulled on the door handle again. "Ryan, open the door, honey."

When the panels didn't budge, Jason growled low and raced down the steps. He ran around the side of the building to the broken window. Avoiding the jagged pieces of glass was a challenge, but Jason was determined to get inside the monastery. Something whispered in his ear that Ryan was in trouble, and Jason wasn't going to let his lover deal with those crazy spirits on his own, even if Jason couldn't really help. He could lend moral support if nothing else.

The chill of the room settled into Jason's flesh as he entered the library. The cold came from something other than the weather. He shuddered, but headed out into the hallway. The kitchen was to his left towards the back of the monastery, yet a feeling seemed to want him to go to the foyer and the staircase.

"Ryan," he called before stalking to the left.

He'd clean up and go after his lover. There wasn't a doubt in his mind that Ryan had come into St. Xavier without him. Fear sparked along his nerves. Going in there unprepared and full of anger probably wasn't the best way for Ryan to approach the spirits. Not that Jason knew anything about fighting ghosts and sending them on their way.

He washed up as quickly as he could, urgency driving him. Grabbing a ragged towel from the pile next to the sink, Jason dried off and tossed it back on the counter before heading to the stairs. He glanced down as he took his first step up and saw a dark smear on the newel post.

Crouching down, he ran his finger over it and it was sticky, meaning it was fresh. It wasn't Hank's because no one having his blood on them had come into the monastery except for Jason, and he hadn't been near the banister until after he'd cleaned up. That meant it had to be Ryan's, unless it was some of the disappearing blood that seemed to exist around the place. He wiped it on his jeans and straightened.

"Ryan? Are you in here? Where are you?" Jason shouted as he took the stairs two at a time.

No one answered him, yet something told him Ryan was in the monastery and not outside. A decaying stench reached his nose when he got to the second floor landing. Bending, Jason breathed through his mouth, trying to ignore the smell. He remembered the nuns of the monastery had supposedly died the day before anyone found them. Could the odour filling the hallway be from their dead bodies?

Blinking and clearing his vision, he spotted Ryan lying on the floor in front of the first door. His T-shirt was wrapped around his head with blood slowly seeping through the thin fabric. So the blood at the bottom of the stairs was Ryan's. Jason rushed over and dropped to his knees next to him. Apparently the stench had got to Ryan because there was a pile of vomit nearby.

"Ryan, are you okay?"

Jason rolled the slender man over onto his back, careful not to shake him. He didn't know how badly Ryan was hurt and didn't want to cause any more injuries. After unwinding the T-shirt from around Ryan's head, Jason saw there were several bruises and two large cuts.

"Honey, are you okay? Can you hear me?" He shook Ryan's shoulder gently. "Come on, Ryan. I need you to talk to me, so I know you're okay."

The temperature dropped around them, chilling Jason until his breath appeared as he exhaled. Gooseflesh covered his skin and rage overwhelmed him. He closed his eyes and inhaled sharply. Every instinct told him to grab Ryan and get the hell out of the monastery, but he wasn't willing to run away, even though he didn't know what the fuck he was doing.

"I'm not going to run from you. Not until I know Ryan's all right." He trailed his fingers over Ryan's cheek. "Please wake up. We have to get out of here before something worse happens."

The rustle of clothing drew Jason's attention to where the staircase continued up to the third floor. Darkness swirled, spanning the entire width of the hallway. Something moved within that blackness and Jason's stomach clenched with fear. He rested his trembling hand on Ryan's chest while keeping his gaze pinned on the shadows.

"I don't know what happened, but you can't have him. I'm taking him out of here."

Without waiting, he scooped Ryan up and sprinted down the stairs. Footsteps chased him and, though Jason was tempted, he didn't look over his shoulder to see who it was. They needed to get out right then because whatever had attacked Ryan seemed more than willing to do it again.

When he hit the first floor, he skidded as he rounded the corner and went right to the library. Instead of trying to climb out of the broken window, he struggled to open the French door leading out into the garden. He slipped through and slammed it shut, managing not to drop Ryan in the process.

Don't look back, his brain told him as he rushed to the cottage. Jason felt the hate-filled gaze of someone burning between his shoulder blades. As he reached the porch, the door swung open.

"Hey, big boss, what's up?"

Jason jumped and scrambled to keep his footing as his personal assistant stepped out of the cottage. "Roland, what the fuck are you doing here?"

Roland's hazel eyes widened at the sight of an unconscious Ryan in Jason's arms. Moving to the side, he opened the door wider and gestured for Jason to go inside. "Apparently, I'm going to play nurse."

Ryan moaned, and Jason's concern focused on his lover. He laid the injured man on the couch.

"Get me the first aid kit! It's under the sink in the bathroom."

"Right."

Jason settled on the couch next to Ryan's hip, stroking Ryan's face without touching the bruises or cuts. "Ryan, come on. Open those pretty eyes for me."

Ryan's eyelashes fluttered for a second before opening to stare blankly at Jason. His lips moved, but Jason couldn't hear what he said. Leaning forward, he got close to Ryan and frowned.

"So much blood. Terrible death. No eyes. Why don't they have any eyes? So much pain." Tears welled in, and spilled from, Ryan's eyes. "They're so angry, Jason. We have to help them."

Jason eased back and grimaced. "I don't think we can help them. It might be better if we just raze this place to the ground and sow the land with salt or something."

"No." Ryan grabbed Jason's arm and squeezed hard enough to whiten the skin under his fingers. "We can't leave them trapped like that. We have to find out the truth. There's too much evil and rage in there to just ignore it."

"Here you go, Jason."

Ryan started as Roland walked up behind Jason. "Who are you?"

"I'm Roland Harkin, Jason's personal assistant extraordinaire." Roland smiled at Ryan. "You must be the priest that's got Jason all hot and bothered."

"Now really isn't the time, Roland," Jason admonished.

A crash of thunder caused all three of them to jump. Jason glanced up at the ceiling as rain started hitting the roof.

"Shit. I need to go get that window covered over at the monastery before rain gets inside and ruins the floor."

"Don't go over there by yourself. It's not safe anymore, Jason. They're all gaining power and getting stronger.

Hurting Hank and me is just the beginning. That's why we need to free them of the monastery." Ryan struggled to sit up, whimpering slightly as he lifted his head.

"No. I'm not leaving you alone. Roland will stay with you while I board up the place. I should have asked one of the men to stay and help me, but they weren't too eager to stick around." Jason rubbed the back of his neck in frustration. He didn't really want to go back to the monastery on his own, but if he didn't, there could be more damage done.

"But…" Ryan protested.

Roland chuckled, even as he pushed Jason to the side so he could reach Ryan's wounds. "Lucky for you, I didn't come down here by myself, though I'd decided I needed to see for myself what was going on here. You started to sound extremely stressed on the phone every time I called. Also, I knew I'd go crazy if I did. I brought my latest with me. Burt will be back in a minute. He went to get our luggage. He can go with you to take care of that window while I tend to your boyfriend."

Jason didn't really care why Roland and his companion came down, though he was happy to see them. All he wanted was to get things taken care of at the monastery and make sure Ryan was okay. After that, they would discuss not only Roland's presence, but what they should do about the spirits terrorising the place. He pushed to his feet and turned as a tall blond guy stepped into the room.

"You must be Burt. Roland said he brought you along. Can you come with me and help board up a broken window?"

"Sure." Burt strolled over and brushed a kiss over the top of Roland's head. "We'll be back in a few, sweetheart."

The man was huge. Burt had to stand at least six-foot five. Dressed in an old pair of jeans and a heavy metal T-shirt, the man looked nothing like Roland's usual. The hair was right though. Roland always did have a thing for ex-military men. There was something about the short haircut and commanding attitude of such men that turned Roland on.

"You ready?" Burt prompted.

"Yeah. Sorry."

They dashed through the rain to the monastery and managed to cover the window without any more incidents. Burt didn't speak and Jason wasn't interested in chatting. All he wanted at the moment was to get back to the relative safety of the cottage.

* * * *

Ryan winced as Roland dabbed at his head with an alcohol-soaked cotton ball. He wondered how close Roland and Jason really were. Although Jason had told Ryan there was nothing sexual going on with his assistant, Ryan couldn't believe Jason could be around the gorgeous man on a daily basis without desiring him.

"I know what you're thinking," Roland said around an amused smile.

"You do?"

"Yes, I do. You're wondering why Jason hasn't snapped me up. Well, truth is, he tells me I'm too high maintenance."

New to relationships, Ryan needed to ask Roland to clarify his statement.

Roland set the bloodied cotton balls on the table and turned Ryan's head from side to side. "You could probably use a couple of stitches."

Ryan shook his head. Because he was no longer under the umbrella of the church, he didn't have the insurance or money required for an emergency room visit. "Can you just put bandages on them?"

"I can, but they'll probably scar."

Ryan shrugged. "I've never been a beauty anyway."

Roland gasped, dramatically putting his hand to his mouth. "You're kidding, right? Is this some kind of priest thing? Do they train you not to see the beauty staring back at you in the mirror?"

Ryan didn't want to talk about his looks. For someone who had always felt ugly on the inside, the outside had never mattered to him. He was more interested in hearing about how to avoid losing Jason. "So, what did you mean when you said that you were too high maintenance for Jason?"

Roland fastened a bandage over one of the cuts on Ryan's forehead. "Oh, you know, I like to have a man cater to me. It's not that I can't do things for myself, but why should I when I can get someone to do it for me. You know what I'm saying?"

Ryan shook his head. He'd always done things for himself. "I don't think I do, but even so, why doesn't Jason like to do things for you?"

After applying the last bandage, Roland started putting the supplies back into the first aid box. "It's not that he doesn't like to do them, he just knows I'm not as helpless as I pretend." He shrugged. "It's other things too."

"Such as?"

"I like to hear how gorgeous I am," Roland began.

"You are."

Roland flashed Ryan a million dollar smile. "Yes, I know, but I still like to hear it. Preferably by someone who's naked and begging to fuck me," Roland said with a wink. "Jason tells me it isn't becoming, but hundreds of men say otherwise."

Ryan made a mental note not to ask Jason to do things for him or fish for compliments. If that's all there was to it, he didn't see a problem. "So how long have you known Burt?"

"Mmm mmm mmm that's one fine man, isn't he? He stopped me last week for going forty-five in a school zone, and I've had him in my bed ever since."

"He's a police officer?" Ryan looked towards the window. The news could either be a blessing or a curse.

"Yeah, he has a huge gun, and let me tell you, he knows how to use it." Roland chuckled at his own joke.

Ryan had never met anyone like Roland. Although the man looked like an angel, Ryan suspected he had a little more devil in him than the average man. By the smile lighting up Roland's face, Ryan suspected it felt like the perfect combination to Roland.

"So enough about me and my hunky cop. What happened to you?"

Ryan closed his eyes and shook his head. He doubted he'd ever forget the images of the murdered nuns. Although Roland seemed like a nice man, Ryan wasn't ready to open himself to the relative stranger. "I think I should go lie down."

Ryan began to leave the room. "Would you tell Jason I need to talk to him when he gets back?"

"Sure." Roland cleared his throat. "Can I ask you something?"

Ryan stopped, but didn't turn to face Roland. He was barely holding himself together and didn't want his frailty known. "Yes."

"It's really haunted, isn't it?"

The lump in Ryan's throat prevented him from speaking. He nodded once before continuing towards the bedroom. His silence lasted until he shut the bedroom door and threw himself onto the bed. All the pain he'd felt from the murdered women burst from him in a body racking sob. He buried his face in the pillow and cried for the innocent souls murdered in such a brutal way.

Ryan heard the door open moments before the bed beside him dipped.

"Hey, hey," Jason soothed.

Strong arms surrounded Ryan and pulled him against a solid chest. For several moments, Jason didn't say anything. He simply gave Ryan the chance to get his emotions under control. "Sorry," Ryan said, taking the tissue Jason held out.

Jason tightened his hold on Ryan. "I don't want you going back in there."

"I have to," Ryan mumbled against Jason's shoulder. "I don't know why, but I know it has to be me." Ryan lifted his head and stared into Jason's eyes. Although it had been such a short time, Jason had come to mean everything to him. The thought of Jason anywhere near the evil inside St. Xavier tore Ryan up inside. "I need you to let me do this alone."

"No. That building's my responsibility, so either I go in with you or you don't go at all." He lifted Ryan until they were eye to eye. "Can you tell me what you saw?"

'I see dead people' seemed a little too clichéd for the situation. "The nuns were mutilated not just killed.

Whoever did it must've hated them for some reason. What I can't work out is why Ann would hate her fellow Sisters so much that she would do something like that."

"What're you saying? You think Sister Ann wasn't the one behind the murders?" Jason asked, his eyebrows drawing together.

Ryan shook his head. "I don't know. I guess I'm just trying to work it out. I mean, I definitely saw Father Clennan push Hank through that window." Ryan rolled over onto his back and stared up at the ceiling. "It would explain why he's not buried with the other priests." He turned his head to look at Jason. "I think I need to get my hands on Father Paul's journals."

* * * *

"Come back to bed," Jason urged.

From his spot beside the window, Ryan looked away from the monastery. It had been hours since he'd gone with Jason to the hospital to check on Hank, and Ryan still couldn't get the bandaged image of the once strong contractor out of his head. "Go back to sleep."

Jason threw off the covers and ran a hand down his torso to settle on his awakening cock. "That's not what I'm in the mood for."

Ryan tried to push away thoughts of the monastery. He'd been awake since their earlier love making session, trying to puzzle out what had really happened at St. Xavier. There was really only one person he could ask who would know the truth, but he doubted Bishop Adler would be forthcoming with any information that would cast the church in a bad light. According to Hank, the hands that pushed him had felt very real. Although he admitted he hadn't seen anyone in the room with him, Hank told the police he had distinctly heard the words, 'Spying will be the death of you'. Hank hadn't elaborated, but Ryan knew it had to do with Hank watching Ryan from the window.

"What's going on? Are you tired of my cock already?" Jason asked with a wicked smile on his gorgeous face.

Ryan unfolded his legs out from under him and pounced on the bed. He straddled Jason's hips and rubbed the crease of his ass against the hard length. "What do *you* think?"

Jason pulled Ryan down for a deep kiss. "Mmmm. I think you seem awfully preoccupied with the horrors going on next door instead of the best parts of life going on right in front of you."

Ryan bit his bottom lip. He couldn't just blurt out the truth, that he doubted he'd make it out of the situation alive, so what? What reason should he give the man for pulling away? Ryan knew it would be hard enough on Jason if, or when, something serious happened to him. But how could he deny what he felt for Jason?

"I don't want to fall for you any harder than I already have," Ryan whispered.

"Why? I'm not good enough?" Jason rose up to rest on his elbows.

Ryan shook his head. "You're the best thing that's ever happened to me." He stared into Jason's eyes, making sure the gorgeous man understood the depths of what he'd just admitted. "But there are things I need to do, and I'm not sure how they'll turn out."

Jason pushed himself into a sitting position and grabbed Ryan's upper arms, giving him a shake. "Are you talking about the monastery? Fuck that building and everyone inside it!" he bellowed. "I don't know what happened fifty years ago, but I won't have anything happen to you because some nun went wacko."

Ryan opened his mouth to speak, but Jason shut him up with another deep kiss. Ryan accepted the probing tongue. Although it had been such a short time, he'd come to love the way Jason kissed him. Jason kissed with his whole body, and Ryan could think of nothing but having the man's cock buried deep inside him. He pushed Jason back and began searching for the bottle of lube they'd used only hours earlier.

"I think it fell off the bed and rolled under it," Jason said, squeezing Ryan's ass.

With an impatient growl, Ryan moved to the edge of the bed. He peered over the side before reaching down. When he began searching blindly for the bottle, he felt the mattress behind him dip. Just as his fingers came into contact with the slippery bottle, he felt a warm tongue slide down the crease of his ass to settle over the well-fucked hole.

"Mmmm," he moaned. He scooted back far enough to brace his forearms on the edge of the mattress and brought his legs up under his torso. The new position allowed Jason's drilling tongue deeper access. "Oh, fuck. I think I've died and gone to heaven."

As soon as the words were out of his mouth, he bit his bottom lip. No. He would not think of death or the monastery while being pleasured by the irresistible man. Turning his attention to the bedside table, Ryan stretched to reach the box of condoms. He fumbled for several moments before eventually retrieving and opening the foil packet that would allow Jason to bury his cock instead of his tongue.

Holding the condom up, Ryan glanced over his shoulder. The sight of Jason's face buried in the crack of his ass stole his voice for several pleasurable moments. "Fuck me," he finally moaned.

Jason scraped his teeth across Ryan's hole once more before taking the condom. "Don't move."

Despite Jason's command, Ryan started to scoot back away from the edge. "Taking a header onto this hardwood floor with the first thrust isn't my idea of a good time."

Jason wrapped an arm around Ryan's chest and pulled him up to his knees. "I won't let you fall," he whispered in his ear. While he spoke, Jason coated Ryan's hole with lube. "I want to feel your body while I fuck you."

Jason guided his sheathed cock to Ryan's entrance while the arm around Ryan's chest tightened. Ryan leant his head back against Jason's shoulder. There were so many positions he'd yet to try. "Show me."

Sliding his cock in deep, Jason's hand trailed around to encircle Ryan's cock while the hand on Ryan's chest moved to pinch his nipple. "I want to teach you everything I've learned about making love."

Ryan moaned as Jason's thick cock began to slide in and out of him. How he'd gone from a virgin to a slut for Jason's cock in less than a week was still a mystery, but Ryan had no intention of questioning his desire. Jason had opened a side of Ryan long buried, and Ryan felt like he was truly alive for the first time in his life.

Jason kissed his way down the column of Ryan's neck to the top of his shoulder before crossing over to his spine. "I want everything when I hold you. Things I don't have a right to."

When Jason's thrusts increased in intensity, Ryan fell forward onto his hands and knees. He was happy to see he was about ten inches from the mattress edge, more than enough room to make him feel safe. Ryan slammed his hips back, impaling himself on Jason's thick length. "Take what you want from me, and I'll happily give you more."

Jason groaned. "Don't promise what you can't deliver."

Ryan gripped the sheets under his hands as Jason fucked him harder. He wanted to tell Jason how he felt about him, but the daunting task still awaiting him inside the monastery stopped him. He might not be able to promise Jason forever, but there was one thing he could promise with no reservations. "As long as I'm here, my ass, my heart and my soul are yours."

Jason buried his cock deep and cried Ryan's name. "Mine," he growled, before biting down on Ryan's shoulder blade.

The ownership the word evoked triggered Ryan's orgasm. The first burst of cum sneaked up on him, and Ryan's body bucked at the overwhelming sensation. His skin broke out in gooseflesh as he rode out his climax with Jason still buried deep inside him.

In unison, they toppled to the bed, the top of Ryan's head hanging over the edge of the mattress. Whether it was selfishness talking or fear, Ryan wasn't sure, but he knew he would put off going back into the monastery for a few more days. He wanted more time with the man whose weight made him feel safer than he'd ever felt. The spirits had haunted St. Xavier for over fifty years, they could wait until he had lived more of the life he would soon be risking.

Chapter Nine

The smell of bacon woke Ryan. He rolled to Jason's side of the bed, seeking warmth. When he met nothing but cold sheets, Ryan opened his eyes to find Jason gone.

Flipping over onto his back, Ryan stretched his arms over his head and winced. It felt as though there wasn't a single muscle in his body that wasn't sore. Whether it was from the enthusiastic sex or the fall down the staircase, he wasn't sure.

Ryan began to tick off the things he needed to accomplish for the day. First and foremost, he needed to find a church that would accept him the way he was. His thoughts strayed towards the gardens surrounding St. Xavier. The work done to prune and clean out the long-forgotten flower beds had done wonders. It was almost as if God was trying to compensate for the evil going on inside with a fresh explosion of colours and blooms. Perhaps a few hours praying amongst nature would settle his soul.

His attention was drawn to loud voices outside. Ryan rolled out of bed and walked to the window. Below, Jason and Roland were having some sort of argument. After shaking his head emphatically, Jason turned away and walked in the direction of the monastery.

"No!" Ryan yelled. He grabbed the sheet off the bed and ran out of the bedroom. By the time he made it down the stairs, he had the sheet wrapped around him toga-style. "Excuse me," he said to Burt on his dash through the living room. Once outside, Ryan yelled again. "Jason!"

Hearing Ryan, Jason stopped and turned around. "Go back into the house."

Ryan finally caught up and flung himself at the man who meant everything to him. "Don't go in there," he pleaded. Although he was still twenty yards from the monastery, gooseflesh rose on Ryan's skin.

Jason wrapped his arms around Ryan and brought him against his chest. "I didn't plan on it."

Surprised, Ryan tilted his chin up and gazed into Jason's eyes. "Then what're you doing?"

"He's shutting down the renovations," Roland answered, coming up behind Ryan.

The announcement was music to Ryan's ears. "You are?"

Jason nodded. "I won't take any more chances until I know it's safe. I'm going to meet with the contractors and see if I can reschedule the work for a later time."

"It's going to cost him a fortune," Roland started to argue.

"Better money than lives, Roland," Jason countered.

Although Ryan hated the idea of Jason jeopardising his business, he was secretly pleased. He buried his face against Jason's neck and hugged him tighter. "Thank you."

"For what?" Jason asked, tilting Ryan's chin up for a quick kiss.

"For giving me more time." Ryan threaded his fingers through Jason's hair and pulled him down for a deep kiss. As always, the kiss ignited Ryan's newly freed libido, hardening his cock in a matter of seconds.

When Jason maneuvered his muscled thigh between Ryan's legs, Ryan took full advantage and began grinding himself towards climax. It was Roland's laughter that threw a bucket of ice water on his desire.

"Although I'm enjoying this little scene more than any porn I've ever watched, you might like to know that a truck is coming up the driveway," Roland said, his laughter dying down.

Ryan broke the kiss and immediately tried to separate himself from Jason. It was then he noticed the sheet was already on the ground at his feet. Embarrassed beyond measure, Ryan scooped up the sheet and ran towards the house.

"It's okay. Don't worry about it," Jason yelled.

Ryan shut the door and collapsed against it, still clutching the sheet around his waist. "I can't believe that just happened."

From his position by the window, Burt shrugged. "I doubt the guys in the truck saw anything."

Ryan turned his head to address Burt. It was obvious by the hard length straining against the man's jeans that he'd not only witnessed Ryan's embarrassment but, like Roland, had enjoyed the show. Shaking his head, Ryan walked towards the stairs. "I'm gonna go hide in shame now."

"Why?" Burt asked. "From my vantage point, you have nothing to be ashamed of. It's nice to see two men so into each other they forget the world around them."

Ryan shook his head. Coming off as a scared virgin wasn't his goal, but the description wasn't far from the truth. "I'm new to all this."

Burt nodded. "Roland told me you just left the Church. Your reasons must've been pretty damn important to you to give up everything."

Ryan's gaze automatically went to the window. Jason was outside talking to several men. "Yeah. Although the way I've been behaving lately, a person would be hard-pressed to identify me as a deacon."

Burt cleared his throat and took a step forwards. "I'm not trying to get into your business or anything, but from what Roland tells me, Jason's extremely comfortable with sex. Hell, he's built his entire fortune on it. If you're not comfortable in his world, you should either get out or get over it."

Ryan started up the stairs. He knew Burt was right. Ryan paused on the steps. He needed to start thinking of himself and his future in spiritual terms. He'd never be comfortable with sex if he continued to think like a Catholic Deacon. Resigning his position was only the first step. It was important that he stopped being so hard on himself. Ryan doubted anyone would expect him to put aside the Catholic teachings he'd clung to for so many years overnight. One step at a time, he reminded himself as he continued up the staircase.

* * * *

After a quick shower and change of clothes, Ryan went out the back door of the cottage to the garden. Jason was still negotiating with his various contractors, so Ryan thought it would be the perfect time to find a place to reflect.

He wandered the gardens, stopping to appreciate the profusion of colours swaying in the slight breeze. The deeper into the garden he went, the calmer he felt. Maybe this was all the church he needed?

Ryan shook his head. The thought went against everything he'd been raised to believe. He found a small hexagon of thick green grass surrounded by yellow and lavender blooms. The profusion of wildflowers found in an otherwise manicured and highly designed garden surprised him.

Rubbing his chest, Ryan stepped into the hidden garden that seemed to call to him. The morning dew had quickly evaporated, leaving the plush grass soft and comforting. Ryan lay down on his back and stared up at the cloudless sky. "Is this where I'm meant to be?"

In a voice as soft as the blades of grass under him, Ryan continued. "Did you send me into the monastery to test me or punish me? I know I'm going against the Church in my relationship with Jason, but he makes me feel things I've never experienced before. In my heart, I know you wouldn't have blessed me with these feelings if I wasn't meant to explore them. It doesn't mean I'm any less devoted to you. As a matter of fact, the closer I come to falling in love, the more beauty I'm able to see in the world around me. Was that your plan for me?"

Ryan sighed. He didn't expect an immediate answer. He truly believed God guided him in other ways. Leaving the church was the path he was meant to take, he had no doubt about that, but what now? Where would his new life lead him? What was he meant to do?

Something off to the side caught his eye. Ryan rolled his head over enough to look at the object straight on and gasped. *Sister Ann.* He knew without a doubt it was the murderous nun staring down at him from the fourth floor. She wasn't covered in blood as others had described her. Instead, Ann appeared freshly bathed and…heartbroken. *Strange.* It wasn't until she took a step back that more pieces of the puzzle fell into place.

Ryan got to his feet and held his hands up towards the window, wishing he could help the solemn woman without venturing inside the monastery.

Ann placed her palm against the window. The gesture was neither frightening nor threatening. It was as if she were reaching out to Ryan.

"You out here?" Jason called, breaking into the profound moment.

Ryan briefly took his eyes away from the window, and when he looked back, Sister Ann was gone. "Wait!" he called. He suddenly felt an emptiness he couldn't begin to explain. Ryan collapsed back on the grass with tears in his eyes.

"There you are." Jason stepped into the garden and looked down at Ryan.

Ryan brushed away the errant tears in the hope Jason wouldn't see them.

"Hey, what's wrong?" Jason sat beside Ryan and pulled him into his lap.

"I saw her."

"Who?"

"Sister Ann," he answered, pointing up to the window. "What if we're wrong about her?"

Jason shook his head. "I'm sorry, babe, but I'm not following you."

Ryan looked away from the window. "She was pregnant."

Jason's entire body immediately stiffened. "Are you sure it was Sister Ann? Because I gotta say, the woman who came after me with hatred in her eyes wasn't pregnant."

"I'm sure." Ryan nuzzled his face against Jason's shoulder. "She wanted me to know. Why, I'm still not sure, but I know it's important."

"Surely Bishop Adler would've known if one of the nuns was pregnant. Maybe we should pay him a visit."

Ryan shook his head. "He won't tell us the truth. He wouldn't do anything to tarnish the Church's reputation. However, if you could distract him long enough for me to sneak into his office, maybe I can get my hands on the truth."

"How so?"

"Father Paul kept journals and, for whatever reason, Bishop Adler removed everything prior to nineteen sixty-nine. I have a feeling that everything we need to know is in those journals."

"So how do we get them?" Jason asked.

"*That* is a good question."

* * * *

Ryan picked at the food on his plate. He wished he could figure out a different plan, but he and Jason had gone over and over different scenarios and the one they'd come up with seemed like the most logical.

The idea of subjecting Jason to Bishop Adler's wrath and condemnation didn't sit well. He glanced up from his barely-touched lunch to see three sets of eyes staring at him. "What?"

"Do you know how many people would kill to get a taste of my chicken marsala?" Roland asked, disappointment clearly written on his down-turned mouth.

"Sorry. It's not your cooking, I promise. I'm sure any other time I'd have moved on to seconds by now. It's just..."

"We know," Jason said, reaching over to clasp Ryan's hand. "The situation's getting to all of us. Hopefully you'll find those journals and we can put this bullshit behind us."

Jason's statement brought up an entirely new set of questions. Ryan squeezed Jason's hand. "What will you do if St. Xavier can't be cleansed? I mean, I'll die trying, but what happens if it doesn't work?"

Jason threw his fork down and pushed his chair back. The next thing Ryan knew he was being hoisted out of his chair and positioned on Jason's lap. "Let's get something straight right here and now. If it comes to it, I'll tear that fucking place down before I'll risk losing you. You got that?"

"Yes, but Roland's made it perfectly clear that the loss of such an investment could ruin you financially. What then? Where will you go?"

Jason glared at Roland. "He had no business telling you that."

Roland quickly excused himself under the guise of cleaning the table.

"Don't be angry with Roland. He only said something because he cares about you." Ryan cupped Jason's cheek. "You're lucky to have people like that in your life."

Jason closed his eyes and leant in to Ryan's touch. "I know." Jason turned his head and kissed Ryan's palm. "Losing St. Xavier will set me back, I won't deny that, but I started my company with absolutely nothing but a dream." Jason pulled Ryan in for a short, but deep, kiss. "I still have that dream. Nothing can stop me when I set my mind to something."

Tired of beating around the bush, Ryan asked the real question that had hovered over them since their first night together. "What about me? If you move away will I ever see you again?"

Instead of an immediate answer, Jason put his hands on Ryan's ass and stood. Ryan quickly wrapped his legs around Jason's waist as he was carried to the small kitchen.

"Roland, tell Ryan what I told you this morning."

Roland turned off the faucet and reached for a dish towel. "That if Burt and I were going to engage in wild sex to please try and not destroy the wall behind the bed?"

Jason blew out an exasperated breath. "No. Tell him what I told you I'd do if I had to abandon St. Xavier."

Roland's face brightened. "Oh! Sorry." Roland stared into Ryan's eyes. "Jason said he'd take you and go back to the flagship resort outside of Napa."

"Thank you," Jason said. He turned around and carried Ryan out of the kitchen and to the living room.

"Did you mean it?" Ryan asked, peppering Jason's face with kisses.

"Of course I meant it." Jason sat on the sofa with Ryan still in his arms.

"But, I thought…I mean…you could probably have your pick of men."

Jason settled Ryan further back on his legs until the two of them were looking at each other. "I've spent the majority of my adult life devoted to making piles of money. I won't lie, there've been a lot of men in my bed along the way, but none of them meant more to me than my work."

Ryan opened his mouth to ask where he fitted in, but Jason put his index finger over Ryan's lips.

"It hit me this morning when I was outside arguing with Roland. Suddenly, losing the money I've invested in St. Xavier didn't matter to me as much as keeping you with me. That's a first for me." Jason's fingertip traced the ridge around Ryan's lips. "I've never been with anyone like you, and I'm not willing to give you up. I probably never will."

Although it wasn't a declaration of love, the sentiment was closer than Ryan could ever have hoped to hear from the man of his dreams. Ryan was tempted to ask Jason to just run away with him and forget St. Xavier, but he knew he couldn't do that. His gut told him it was important to finish what he'd started in the monastery. His own declaration would have to come later once the rubble settled. Only then would he be able to fully give himself to the man he'd fallen in love with.

"I hate to break up the lovefest, but Adler should be here in about ten minutes," Roland said, coming into the room.

Jason ignored Roland and stared into Ryan's eyes. "Are you sure you want to do this?"

Ryan nodded. "Yeah. I hate to put you through it, but I'll need as much time as you can give me. Once I find the journals and get out of the house, I'll call you."

"Just be careful. We both know you need to do this, but make sure no one sees you breaking in."

"I won't have to. I have a key."

* * * *

Jason watched Ryan drive away, fighting back the urge to run after him and stop his lover from going.

"Don't do it."

He turned to look at Burt standing next to him. "Don't do what?"

"Don't try to protect him by smothering him. He's an adult, and he won't appreciate you locking him away, even if you do it out of love." Burt shrugged. "I know the look. I've seen other guys wear it when their loved ones were heading into what could be a dangerous situation. Of course, I've probably worn it a time or two myself."

Jason gestured for Burt to follow him back to the cottage. "It's not that I don't think Ryan can take care of himself. It's more this feeling I have that Ryan would willingly give up his life to free the spirits in this place. I don't want him to do that. I want him to stay alive. We have a lot of years left to spend together."

"True, but how do you know cleansing this place isn't what Ryan was born for in the first place? Maybe his destiny is tied up with the history of this building."

"Do you know something I don't?" Jason frowned.

Burt shook his head. "I don't know anything more about this place than what Roland told me. I'm just saying we can't stop a person from fulfilling his destiny, no matter what it is."

Jason grimaced but didn't reply. He didn't think he cared whether ridding the monastery of its ghosts was Ryan's destiny or not. All he wanted was his lover safe and not tormented by what, or who, existed in that place. Roland met them at the door.

"Turn around, boss. The honorable Bishop Adler is at the gate, and he doesn't sound happy about being asked to come here." Roland grinned.

"If he didn't want to come, he could have told me no, or had me meet him at the diocese's house, though that would have defeated the purpose of getting him here." Jason straightened his shoulders and tugged on his cuffs. "How do I look?"

"You're kidding, right?" Roland grabbed Jason and turned him around, giving him a small shove towards the front gate. "You look fine and it's not like you're asking the dear bishop for Ryan's hand in marriage, jackass. You're creating a diversion so your ex-priest of a boyfriend can steal some journals from the man."

"Great, not only have I corrupted Ryan carnally, I've corrupted his morals about stealing." Jason muttered as he stuffed his hands in his pockets and started walking away.

Roland and Burt's laughter drifted on the breeze like it was following him.

"I'll buzz him in," Roland called and Jason waved a hand in acknowledgement.

As he wound his way along the garden paths, he wondered what he should talk to Adler about, not sure if bringing up Ryan's desertion of his vows was a good idea. He glanced up at the stone building, his gaze drawn to the fourth floor windows. Jason stumbled to a halt when he spotted the nun framed in the corner window. The front of her habit glistened like the blood soaking it was still wet. He could see the anguish in her green eyes, even though he knew he should have been too far away to see anything. Something squirmed in the back of his mind, yet he couldn't force it into the light. Whatever it was would come to him eventually.

Bring him to me!

The angry demand knifed through Jason's brain, threatening to drive him to his knees.

"Who?" He asked aloud, feeling slightly foolish about talking to himself.

Him.

Fuck! Could the ghost be more cryptic? How the hell was he supposed to know who 'him' was?

The slam of a car door shook him out of the trance he'd slipped into. *Damn.* He'd forgotten about the bishop. Shooting another glance up at the windows, he noticed the spirit was gone but darkness blackened the windows on all the lower floors. Shadows that couldn't be penetrated by the setting sun.

Jason rushed around the side of the monastery and strolled up to where an older man stood. He didn't miss the look of disgust the bishop sent his way. Well, he'd known Adler wouldn't be completely happy with meeting him, but Jason had dealt with homophobic bastards before and it didn't matter that this one happened to be a man of God. They were all the same underneath.

"Bishop Adler, thank you for agreeing to meet me here. I didn't want to leave the site unattended. Not with all the construction equipment around for thieves to steal." He held out his hand.

The bishop ignored his gesture, keeping his own hands folded in front of him. "Your assistant didn't really give me a chance to decline, Mr. Bentley. He's a rather forceful young man, which surprises me."

"Why would it surprise you?" Jason narrowed his eyes. "Did you believe all gay men were limp wristed wussies who could be easily cowed by you?"

"I'm sure I had no idea what your kind would be like. I've never had any reason to meet any." Bishop Adler changed the subject. "Why did you need me to come out here?"

"I wondered if you could give me some more background on St. Xavier. I wanted to incorporate some of the history of the place in the resort I'm building."

Bishop Adler drew his indignation tight around him. "Yes, I've heard around town how you're proposing to use St. Xavier. You would desecrate the sanctity of this monastery by using its past in your disgusting hedonistic pursuits? How dare you, Mr. Bentley. Terrible tragedies happened here, and you have no right to use those incidents for your own personal gain."

"What kind of tragedies, Bishop Adler? See, that's what I wanted to know about. I thought maybe I could advertise this place as haunted. Paranormal trips are all the rage right now, even among my kind." He managed to keep his tone even. "I can charge even more for a place with a dark history."

"You are an evil man, Mr. Bentley. What kind of human being would profit from the suffering of others?" Bishop Adler turned to head back to the waiting vehicle. "I refuse to stand here and allow you to destroy the memory of the good man who died here."

Jason reached out, snagging the bishop's sleeve and pulling the man to a halt. "What about the good women who died here? Shouldn't you be as upset about me mocking their memories and reputations as you are about the priest?"

"I am angered about this whole thing, Mr. Bentley. I wasn't in favour of the church selling the monastery. I advocated destroying the entire building and using the land for a cemetery, but the others wanted to recoup some of their losses. They sold St. Xavier to you behind my back. Now I'm going to leave, and don't bother me again. I have nothing else to say about this place."

A large crash came from the monastery and Jason saw Adler pale as a shrill scream sliced through the air, drawing shivers from Jason.

"So you don't want to discuss the spirits that haunt the monastery and why they happen to be stuck there?"

"No!"

Adler turned quickly on his heel and stalked towards his car. Jason scrambled to think of something else to mention. Ryan hadn't called him yet to let him know he'd got the journals and was out of the house.

"What about Deacon Christopher, Bishop Adler? Aren't you worried about Ryan entering the monastery, especially with his history of spirits?"

Bishop Adler froze, but didn't turn to look at Jason. "I'm deeply disappointed in Mr. Christopher. After all the help I gave him, he turned his back on me and the Church to pursue abominations. I blame you for luring him away from the right path. If you hadn't chased after him, he would have been happy to pledge his life to the Church."

"After all the help you gave him?" Jason tilted his head. "I'm puzzled about that comment. What kind of help did you give him? You taught him to be ashamed of himself. You and the Church told him that every true feeling he had was wrong. When he came to you about the spirits he'd encountered as a child, you denied they existed. Where is the help in that?"

Bishop Adler whirled on him, advancing with stiff steps and a snarl. "I did what was best for Ryan at the time. He would have been ridiculed and reviled by society. I gave him a safe place to hide while becoming a strong person by not giving into his vile urges."

Jason didn't back up. He wasn't about to show any sign of fear in front of Adler. "I don't know who you're calling vile. Don't you think God would rather he be truthful about himself? If you're not honest about all aspects of your life, it makes it easy to lie about things. I've always believed God doesn't care who I love as long as I'm not hurting anyone because of it."

"How dare you speak for God? You don't know God, you unholy disgusting man. You've taken what was pure and soiled him with your touch. I should have been more forceful with Ryan. I should have made him take his vows when I thought he was ready. I was too soft with him because of his past."

"You mean because of his step-father and that child molester ghost?" Jason had never seen anyone so angry.

"No…" Adler stopped and his eyes widened. "Of course, I meant those events. What else did you think I meant?"

Adler was backtracking. He hadn't meant just Ryan's unusual childhood and the ghosts. He had meant something else, but before Jason could call him out on that, the phone in his pocket rang. After stepping away from the bishop, he tugged it out and hit the button.

"Bentley."

"I'm out of the house, but there's a problem with the journals. How are things going?" Ryan sounded breathless and excited.

"As well as could be." Jason shot a look over at Adler. "What's going on?"

"I'll tell you when I get there. I'm on my way home."

Jason heard the car start. "Okay. Take it easy and I'll see you when you get here."

"Love you," Ryan said before hanging up.

Jason stared at his phone, wondering if he'd heard right. Wasn't it too early to say the 'L' word? He didn't know the protocol for that since he'd never been in love with any of the men he slept with. Yet if being willing to give up St. Xavier and all the money he'd put into it to keep Ryan safe was love, Jason would shout it from the rooftop. After the whole ghost thing was taken care of, of course.

He put his phone away and turned to smile at Bishop Adler. "You know what, Bishop. You might be right. Maybe I should re-think the course of my sin and rededicate my life to the Church. I have your number if I need any counselling for my offensive homosexual needs. Thank you for coming out tonight."

Jason ushered a stunned Adler to his car and waved as the man drove off. He jogged back to the cottage, bursting in with a yell.

"Ryan's on his way back."

Roland and Burt looked up from where they were snuggled on the couch. Jason dropped into the chair across from them and shook his head.

"Can't you two keep your hands off each other for an hour or two?"

Roland's eyebrows shot up. "Why should we? You certainly couldn't keep your hands off Ryan long enough for the man to recover from hitting his head."

"Touché. I have to say that I don't plan on ever going to the Catholic Church in this town. Bishop Adler might douse me with holy water if he gets anywhere near me again."

"That bad, huh?" Burt shifted Roland slightly on his lap to be able to see Jason clearly.

"The guy's a nutcase and sets a bad example if he wants to convert people to Catholicism."

They heard a car pull in a few minutes later. Jason stood and crossed to the front door to greet Ryan. It was clear from the grim expression on Ryan's face the entire exercise hadn't gone as planned. "What happened?"

Chapter Ten

Getting into Bishop Adler's house wasn't a problem. Evidently the man was so sure he'd seen the last of Ryan he hadn't bothered to change his locks. Upon entering the house, Ryan stopped just inside the door to greet Bishop Adler's long-time companion, Chaucer. He scratched the small Beagle behind the ears for several moments before proceeding towards the office.

Stepping into the dark, panelled room, Ryan took a deep breath. Although it was warm outside, the room smelled of a fire. Perhaps the smoke odour had permeated the heavy drapes and rugs after years of use. Ryan mentally shrugged and walked over to the desk. Bishop Adler liked to hand out his words of wisdom and admonishments from behind the over-sized carved behemoth.

Ryan scanned the top of the desk before starting in on the drawers. A sound from the hallway startled him. Ryan quickly got to his feet and stepped away from the desk just as Ellen Fitzroy came into the room carrying a bucket. The moment she spotted him, she stopped short.

"Deacon Christopher?"

"Hello, Ms. Fitzroy." He tried to keep the fear of being caught from his voice. "I thought you were off today?"

Ryan had known Ellen as long as he'd known Bishop Adler. The woman had to be in her mid to late seventies. The idea that she was still cooking and cleaning for the bishop astounded him.

"Joseph made a mess in the fireplace yesterday, burning some old books. He asked me to come in and tidy his office." Ellen crossed to the fireplace. "May I ask what you're doing here? Joseph told me the two of you had severed your relationship."

Ryan's heart skipped a beat as his gaze swung to the fireplace. "Are those Father Paul's journals?"

Ellen lifted the screen and set it to the side of the fireplace. "Yes. They were nothing but the ramblings of an old man. Joseph considered throwing them out with the garbage, but I told him it would be better to put the fireplace to use."

Ellen rarely spoke unless prompted to do so. He wouldn't call her sour, but she'd never been overly friendly towards him. The fact that she was carrying on a conversation with him was definitely odd. "Did Bishop Adler tell you why we argued?"

On her knees, Ellen scooped a pile of burned paper into the ash bucket. "Yes." She narrowed her eyes as she looked up at Ryan. "You've hurt him a great deal. Joseph has done everything for you, and you repaid his kindness by throwing your perversions in his face."

"No. I'll always be grateful for Bishop Adler's guidance, but I felt it was important to be honest with myself, him and the Church."

Ellen stood and dusted her hands on her apron. "I told him years ago that you would be trouble. You're no different than your mother."

Ryan was shocked by the revelation as well as the vehemence in Ellen's voice. "You knew my mother?"

"Of course. She, like you, carried evil in her heart. Joseph tried his best to guide her along the righteous path, but she turned her back on the church." Ellen's lip lifted in a sneer. "You're no longer welcome in this house. I'd suggest you leave before Joseph returns. Seeing you here…well, Joseph has suffered enough."

Ryan couldn't get his feet to move. He was standing in a room with the only person who'd ever acknowledged knowing his mother, and he wanted answers. "Do you know where my mother is now?"

Ellen turned her back on Ryan and once again began cleaning the fireplace. It was obvious he was being dismissed, but Ryan wasn't going anywhere. "Why didn't Bishop Adler ever tell me he knew my mother?"

When Ellen continued to ignore him, something snapped inside Ryan. He rushed forwards and pulled the old woman to her feet, knocking the bucket of ash over in the process. "Tell me!" he yelled, shaking her by the shoulders.

Ellen's eyes narrowed to mere slits. "I wouldn't do that if I were you."

Ryan glanced down and noticed the wrought iron poker clutched in Ellen's hand. From the look in her eyes, he had no doubt the woman would use the weapon with little thought of the outcome. He released Ellen and took a step back, ready to throw up his arms to protect himself if the need arose.

Suddenly he was more afraid of staying in Bishop Adler's home than he was of entering St. Xavier again. Before Ellen had a chance to slam the heavy iron poker over his head, Ryan backed towards the door. "I'll confront Bishop Adler about my mother. *Do* tell him I stopped by."

Climbing into the safety of Jason's car, Ryan kept one eye on the house as he started the engine and pulled away from the kerb. Not only had the journals been destroyed, but he left Bishop Adler's house with even more questions.

* * * *

By the time he reached St. Xavier and parked the car, his fear had turned to anger. Stepping out onto the driveway, the only thing that kept him from screaming his rage was the sight of Jason standing in the doorway.

Ryan wasted no time reaching for his lover for strength. "He knew her," he said just before kissing Jason. As the kiss deepened, Ryan's heart rate climbed for an entirely different reason.

By the time he broke the kiss, his anger had begun to take a backseat to his desire.

"Who knew her? Who's her?"

"My mom," Ryan answered as Jason led him into the house. "Adler knew my mom according to his housekeeper."

"How? Did she say?"

Ryan shook his head and allowed himself to be pulled down onto the couch beside Jason. He glanced at Roland

and Burt before answering. "She just said I was like my mother. Then she told me Bishop Adler had tried to help her like he helped me. Why didn't he ever mention he knew her?"

"I don't know, babe. Did she grow up here?" Jason asked.

Ryan bit his bottom lip. He was ashamed of himself for not knowing more about the woman who had given birth to him. "I don't know. I remember asking her when I was little if I had a grandma. She told me I didn't have anyone but her. A couple months later I didn't even have that."

Jason leant back and pulled Ryan into his arms. "We'll figure it out. Just know you have me now."

"And me," Roland piped up.

"And me as long as Roland lets me stick around," Burt said with a chuckle.

"Thanks." It was hard for Ryan to believe that he felt more connected to the three people in the room than anyone else ever. He wondered if it had something to do with the men accepting him for who he truly was. *Does it matter?* Ryan decided he wouldn't look the proverbial gift horse in the mouth. He would accept the support and companionship with open arms for as long as he was around.

Ryan's contentment was shattered by the ringing phone in his pocket. There were only a handful of people who had Ryan's private number. Since the majority of those people were in the room with him, it left a very short list. "Bishop Adler," he said before pulling the phone out.

"Don't answer it," Jason advised.

"I have to. There are still a lot of answers I need." Ryan gave Jason a quick peck on the lips before answering the call. "Hello?"

"I should call and report you to the police," Adler snarled.

If he hadn't already, Ryan knew it wouldn't happen. For some reason Bishop Adler shied away from getting the police involved in matters of the church. "I had a key, remember? Besides, you never told me I was no longer welcome in your home, just the church."

"What'd you hope to find with all your snooping around?"

"You know exactly what I was looking for. Otherwise you would've never burned them. What did Father Paul confess in his journals that frightened you so much?" Ryan held his breath. He still didn't know if there was anything incriminating in the journals, but it was a chance he was willing to take.

"Nothing that was any of your business," Bishop Adler blustered. "You've scared Ms. Fitzroy to the point that she was shaking when I arrived home."

"Are you sure she was scared? I doubt it. I imagine it was more anger than fear." Ryan decided to push Bishop Adler to his limits. It was a long shot, but he just might rattle the man enough to make him slip up. "By the way, how many years have you been sleeping with her?"

"Who?"

"Who? Are you saying there has been more than one? I was inquiring about your long-running affair with Ellen." Ryan felt Jason's arms tighten around him. He looked up at the man he loved and gave him a reassuring nod.

"How dare you! Ms. Fitzroy has been in the church's employ since the early fifties. The woman grew up working in the best interests of the Catholic Church. She spent years spreading her love at St. Nicholas before I brought her here to work for me."

Pieces of the puzzle began to slide into place. "What do you know about my mother?"

"I refuse to discuss Maria with you. Now, if I didn't make myself clear enough before, let me warn you. You, Ryan Christopher, are no longer welcome in my home, my church or my life. I never want to be contacted by you again, or I will take this matter to the police."

The line went dead, and Ryan lowered the phone to his lap. "I need to look up records from St. Nicholas' Orphanage."

"Why?"

"I believe that's where Bishop Adler met my mother."

* * * *

While Jason searched the internet for clues, Ryan needed the solitude his garden sanctuary provided. As he sat on the soft grass, he stared up at the window where he'd seen Ann the day before.

In his heart, he already knew what Jason would soon verify. Why else would Sister Ann allow him a glimpse of her pregnant form? If what he suspected was true, Ryan was the grandson of Sister Ann. "Is that why God led me here?" he asked the empty window.

With new resolve, Ryan stood and walked towards the monastery. The closer he got, the more determined he became. This was his destiny. If Sister Ann was his grandmother, not only had his mother been cheated but he had as well.

Ryan turned and started to head towards the front door when one of the side French doors opened mysteriously. "Is that an invitation?"

Before entering the house, Ryan crossed himself and whispered a quick prayer. "Sister Ann?" he called, stepping into a large reception room of some kind.

The door behind him shut with unseen force, trapping Ryan in the monastery. "I'm not afraid," Ryan announced. "I know this is where I'm meant to be."

He was met by silence. Ryan carefully made his way to the staircase. Every time he'd seen Sister Ann she'd been on the fourth floor. Would he find her there now? As he passed the second-floor landing, he tried to keep his eyes on the steps in front of him.

"Sister Ann?" he called again to break the eerie silence.

When he reached the third-floor landing, Ryan was knocked to the floor. The dark shape hovering over him morphed into the same face he'd seen push Hank through the office window.

"Father Clennan," Ryan whispered as the misty shape completed its transformation. "Why?"

"I know why you're here." Although Father Clennan's lips didn't move, Ryan heard him perfectly clearly in his head. *"She doesn't deserve eternal peace, and I won't allow you to give it to her."*

Ryan tried to get to his feet but was unable to move. "I don't understand. Why are the two of you still here? You've both been buried."

"I'm here to ensure Sister Ann pays for her crimes."

"By hurting people?" he asked.

"Who are you to judge me?!" Father Clennan bellowed. *"These despicable crimes were not mine. Yet I am the one condemned to watch over her."*

"Condemned by whom?" Ryan remembered Father Clennan's burial plot. "Did the church condemn you for what happened here?"

"I should have been able to stop her, but once the child was taken, all hope was lost." Father Clennan gestured to the row of doors along the third-floor hallway. *"Judge not, lest you see what I saw."*

Ryan tried to close his eyes when the screams began.

"No! You. Will. See!"

Suddenly Ryan's eyes were pinned open by unseen force as the monastery was taken back in time.

Sister Ann appeared from one of the rooms, a bloody cross clutched in her hand. Splattered with blood from head to toe, Sister Ann opened the next door and began screaming. "You saw what he did to me!" she screamed at the cowering nun in the corner. "For nine months you all knew I was locked upstairs. Yet you did nothing."

Ryan gasped as the pointed cross came down on the nun in wild abandon. Over and over, Sister Ann stabbed the woman as she continued to rant.

"You will pay for turning a blind eye while he raped me. You will pay for cowering to the will of that monster. You will pay for sitting idly by while they took my daughter from me!"

Bile rose in Ryan's stomach as Ann gouged the eyes out of the nun. "Dear Lord," he began to pray.

Sister Ann left the nun's room, glistening with a fresh spray of blood. As she started up the steps to the fourth floor, another door opened. Father Clennan stumbled out into the hall. Although it was obvious the priest had already suffered Ann's deadly crucifix, he blindly tried to follow her up the staircase.

When the two apparitions disappeared from view, Ryan wondered why he was still frozen in place. Despite Ann's screams from upstairs, he heard the front door open and close and called out. "Jason! I'm up here."

Footsteps sounded on the steps but Jason didn't answer. It wasn't until he heard the voices that he knew he was still witnessing the past. A much younger Bishop Adler led the way up the steps, followed closely by Father Paul and Ellen Fitzroy.

Dammit! Ryan's gut feeling that Ellen had been involved in some way had been correct.

Bishop Adler ordered Father Paul to stay on the third floor landing as he and Ellen climbed the steps to the fourth floor. Father Paul looked around before bending over to throw up.

Sister Ann's screams intensified even more when Adler and Ellen disappeared from Ryan's view.

"*Shut her up,*" Bishop Adler yelled.

"*You took my baby, you whore!*" Ann screamed.

"*Stop it,*" Father Clennan pleaded, loud enough for Ryan to hear.

"*Stay out of this,*" Bishop Adler ordered.

Moments later a body appeared, tumbling down the steps, grotesque thunks sounding with each strike of Father Clennan's head against the wood. The priest landed a mere foot from Ryan, the dark stain of blood pooling quickly under his head.

Ann's screams continued for several moments before they were suddenly silenced. Ryan's heart was in his throat as he watched Bishop Adler and Ellen Fitzroy make their way down the staircase, sidestepping the small puddles of blood on their way. Ellen was covered in blood, a large knife still in her hand.

"*What happened?*" Father Paul had asked.

"*Sister Ann pushed Father Clennan down the steps. She would have killed the two of us if we hadn't stopped her,*" Bishop Adler explained.

Ryan looked from Bishop Adler to Father Paul. He could tell Father Paul didn't believe the explanation but was too terrified to speak otherwise.

"I understand now," Ryan told Father Clennan's dead body.

Although twisted backwards, Father Clennan's head lifted off the floor to look straight at Ryan. Despite the eyeless sockets, the body spoke. *"Now you see. Sister Ann isn't the only one not finished paying for their crimes."*

"Bishop Adler," Ryan surmised.

"This was his doing. All of it. He's the one who should be here watching over Sister Ann."

"All of it? Including the rape?"

"Yes. I should have gone to the Archbishop, but I wasn't here at the time and Adler assured me Sister Ann was lying. He said the two of them had had an affair and he would spend the rest of his life atoning for his sin." Father Clennan made a gurgling sound. *"I was naïve enough to believe him."*

Ryan was released from the unseen shackles that held him in place. He got to his feet, still looking at Father Clennan's body. "I *will* make it right."

Ryan didn't remember leaving the monastery. One minute he was on the third floor and the next he was standing in front of Jason's door. It took everything he had to turn the knob.

From his position on the couch, Jason looked up from his laptop just as Ryan's world went black.

* * * *

"Have you found anything yet?" Roland asked as he headed towards the kitchen.

Jason shook his head. "No, but I'm getting closer to being able to break into their records. You would think an orphanage would have better firewalls to keep people from getting into their files."

"Are you hacking into their computers?" Burt seemed surprised.

Looking up, Jason grinned. "Yes, Officer. I am. Are you going to arrest me for it?"

"I think I'll go help Roland in the kitchen. If I don't see you doing it, I can't prove you actually did it, right?" Burt stood and followed Roland to the other room.

"Don't worry. I'm not going to take down their server or anything like that. I just want information that everyone seems to want to keep hidden." He typed a little more.

"Why didn't I know you could do this?" Roland looked around the doorframe. "You always make me do the research and shit."

Jason chuckled. "I have to give you something to do to justify that ridiculously large salary I pay you. Besides, I don't usually have the time to do any of that crap. I'm too busy schmoozing the clients."

Roland stuck out his tongue. "Bullshit. You just don't like doing it because it's boring."

"You're probably right." One more tap of the keys and Jason pumped his fist. "I'm in."

Roland raced into the room and dropped onto the couch next to Jason. "What have you found?"

Burt entered a little more slowly. He sat next to Roland and sighed. "I'll try and not get upset by this whole process."

Jason watched as his assistant snuggled close to the cop and whispered something in Burt's ear. Burt blushed while gesturing to Jason.

"Go ahead. Roland's convinced me it's okay for you to do what you're doing."

"Oh really?" Jason quirked an eyebrow. "I can just imagine what he said to convince you."

"Quit teasing my boyfriend." Roland waved at the laptop. "Get digging."

He typed in Ryan's mother's name and, within seconds, he got a hit in the records.

"Hmmm…interesting." He continued scrolling down as he read. "I wonder if that's a connection."

"What?"

Jason got out of the orphanage's records and did a search for Maria Christopher throughout the 'net. Roland reached out and punched him on the arm.

"Hey, what was that for?" He rubbed his biceps.

"You can't just say, 'hmmm…interesting' and not elaborate on it. That's being mean." Roland leant back against Burt and pouted.

"Okay. It appears Maria was raised at St. Nicholas's. She came to the orphanage on June 17, 1962 as a newborn. There's something about that date."

Opening another window, he typed in St. Xavier and the date. When the links popped up, he grunted.

"Oh for God's sake, I should have just done this myself." Roland huffed.

"It would appear that Maria Christopher arrived at St. Nicholas's the day before Sister Ann Cawfield went on her murderous rampage." Jason leant back and stared into space. "Do you suppose Sister Ann might have been Maria's mother? Ryan said he saw Sister Ann in the window and she was pregnant."

"Would the fathers have taken the baby from her because she was a nun and shouldn't have gotten pregnant?" Burt sounded sceptical.

"Hell, I wouldn't put anything past this group of priests. Bishop Adler strikes me as the type of guy who believes anything he did was right because of who he is." Jason clicked on the other tab and saw his search for any more information about Maria Christopher had come up empty. "Damn. Nothing else came up for Maria."

"Do you really think the church would have erased all records of her to cover up what happened at the monastery?"

"I told you, nothing would surprise me with this group of men."

At that moment, the door burst open and Ryan stumbled in, pale and shaken. He froze just inside the cottage and while they watched, his eyes rolled back into his head and he fainted.

"Holy shit!"

Jason shot to his feet and got to Ryan right before he hit the floor. He carried his lover to the couch and sat with him in his arms.

"Ryan, are you okay? What happened to you?" He looked at Roland with a frown. "I'm getting tired of Ryan passing out after being near that fucking building."

"I don't blame you." Roland jumped up and headed to the kitchen again. "I'll get a wet cloth for his forehead. Try to get him to react to you."

Jason kept talking to Ryan, trying to get some response from him. Roland returned with a damp cloth and Jason wiped Ryan's forehead with it. A few minutes later, Ryan's eyelashes fluttered and relief swamped Jason as Ryan met his gaze with sad green eyes.

"The monastery. I know what happened now."

"Why did you go in there by yourself again?" Jason crushed Ryan to his chest. "I don't want you in there without someone else there. You're too vulnerable to them."

"I have to go back, Jason. They need to be free and I know how to do that."

Ryan struggled to sit up, but Jason wasn't willing to let him out of his embrace just yet.

"So what happened?"

"I'm not a hundred percent sure, but I think Bishop Adler raped Sister Ann and got her pregnant. For the nine months of her pregnancy, they locked her away on the fourth floor and I do believe she slowly went mad. They took the baby away from her and she snapped. She killed the nuns one by one because they didn't do anything about the rape." Ryan paused, tears trailing down his face. "Bishop Adler and Ellen killed her to keep everything quiet."

"Well, fuck me," Roland whispered.

Jason shook his head. "I knew there was something twisted about that man, but I'm not sure you should have anything more to do with this situation, Ryan. Maybe we should go to the police and tell them what we know."

"How are you going to explain where all this knowledge came from? I'm sorry, but most police won't believe you when you say spirits showed you the truth." Burt spoke reluctantly.

"To be honest, I think you should leave. Just cut your losses and head to Napa." Roland lifted one of Ryan's arms and pointed to the red marks on Ryan's wrists. "They've physically hurt you, Ryan, and we all know what happened to Hank. It isn't safe for anyone to go in there."

Ryan shook his head, determination evident in every line of his body. "I can't walk away from this. I'm as much a part of the history of the monastery as the others who started the whole tragedy. I'm the only one who can fix it."

"Besides I don't think running away from this will work. It'll haunt you for the rest of your life, Ryan." Burt shrugged when they looked at him. "If he was meant to make this all right, then he can't run away."

"I thought you didn't believe in this stuff." Roland glared at him.

"I said most police wouldn't believe him. I'm not like most of my fellow cops. I'm willing to accept spirits and things we can't see exist in the world." Burt grinned.

"Fine. You're not leaving. So what do you suggest we do? How do we fix this problem?" Jason shifted Ryan slightly, moving the slender man so Jason could see his face.

"We have to get Bishop Adler and Ellen inside the monastery. I think that once they're inside and forced to see what they did, the spirits will be able to move on to whatever Heaven or Hell awaits them." Ryan shuddered. "But more than anything else, Adler and Ellen must face and confess the sins they committed."

Somehow Jason doubted Sister Ann and Father Clennan would be nearly as nice and forgiving as Ryan made them sound. "Okay with me. How do we do that?"

Roland stood. "I'll get us all something to eat before we start plotting the downfall of the bishop."

"I want a shower," Ryan admitted.

"You do that and I want to do some more looking. See if I can find anything else about your mother."

Jason let Ryan stand, making sure Ryan had his balance before letting go of his hand. He watched as the auburn-haired man made his way slowly down the hallway to the bathroom. After the door shut behind Ryan, Jason leant back against the couch and scrubbed his face.

"Since this is going to happen, you and I need to make plans to keep your boyfriend safe."

He met Burt's serious gaze and nodded. "I'm glad you're here."

"So is Roland. He'd be bored to death without me to fuck him."

Shocked laughter exploded from Jason, but he relaxed which seemed to be the result Burt wanted. They started plotting how to keep everyone safe during the next couple of hours.

Chapter Eleven

Jason sat on the couch, watching Ryan pace the living room. Roland and Burt had gone to bed some time earlier, but nothing Jason did could convince Ryan to sleep. Well, almost nothing. Jason had one more trick up his sleeve and he got ready to play it. He didn't want Ryan wearing himself out, because Jason had a feeling tomorrow was going to be the hardest day of Ryan's young life.

"All right. That's enough worrying." He pushed to his feet and swept Ryan into his arms as the younger man walked by him.

"Enough worrying? I'm not worried about anything. I'm just trying to make sure we have everything covered. I don't want one thing to go wrong tomorrow."

"We've done all the planning we can tonight, love. You have to let all the other stuff go because for the most part, you can't control any of it." Jason nuzzled Ryan's hair as he carried him down the hall to their bedroom. "I've got a sure-fire way to get you to relax long enough to fall asleep."

Ryan peered up at him through his eyelashes, a flirtatious grin on his face. "Are you saying sex with you will bore me?"

"I do believe you just issued a dare, Mr. Christopher. Let's see if you feel like running a marathon after I'm done with you."

He shouldered his way into the bedroom and tossed Ryan onto the bed. While Ryan laughed, Jason shut and locked the door before turning to look at his lover. Sprawled across the comforter, Ryan looked sexy as hell with his legs spread and a come-hither smile on his face.

"I think we're overdressed for this to work."

Jason reached up and started opening his shirt, exposing his lightly furred chest one button at a time. Ryan's green eyes widened as Jason finished with his shirt, and moved on to his pants. He took his time, knowing anticipation was just as stimulating as instant gratification. Leaving his pants unzipped, he bent to take off his shoes and socks.

After they were tossed to the side, he turned his back and wiggled his hips, drawing a giggle from Ryan. He glared over his shoulder.

"Are you laughing at my ass?"

Ryan covered his mouth with his hand and shook his head, but his eyes twinkled.

"Oh well, I guess I can deal with a little laughter. Good thing I have other more impressive items for you to feast on, since my butt doesn't seem to inspire you."

Ryan's eyebrows shot up and Jason winked. He'd never felt an urge to tease his lovers like he did now. He peeled off his pants and left them on the floor as he stalked towards the bed.

Holding out his hand, Ryan offered, "Would you like to join me?"

"I'd love to, but you're still clothed and that will never do." Jason crawled onto the bed and straddled Ryan's legs. "I'm more than happy to help you rectify the problem."

Ryan tucked his hands behind his head. "Go right ahead. You seem quite talented in the removal of clothing."

"I've done it a time or two." He grinned as he reached for the waistband of Ryan's jeans. "I can't wait to see what you have under there for me."

"And it is all yours for as long as you want it," Ryan murmured.

Jason paused for a moment to meet Ryan's serious gaze. "Decades. That's how long I'll want it for, and you can have anything of mine you want for just as long."

He leant forward and pressed a kiss to Ryan's lips, plunging his tongue in to tease and play with Ryan's. Whimpering, Ryan cradled the back of Jason's head and applied a little more pressure, taking the kiss deeper.

Thank God he was good at multi-tasking. While he kissed Ryan, Jason managed to get Ryan's jeans undone and slid his hand inside, under Ryan's underwear. He cupped Ryan's cock firmly.

Ryan broke their kiss and arched up into Jason's hand. "Oh!"

"That's it, honey. Let me do all the work tonight. Just lie there and enjoy it."

Not wasting any more time, he stripped Ryan, throwing his clothes over his shoulder, not caring where they ended up. Jason wedged his body between Ryan's legs, his target the erection bobbing in front of his face.

He licked from the base to the tip along the underside of the shaft. Ryan cried out again, and Jason couldn't help but chuckle. He hoped Roland and Burt were sound sleepers because they were in for a long night if they weren't. He swirled his tongue over the head, taking in the pre cum pooling there.

"Jason," Ryan muttered, his hands coming to grip Jason's head tightly. "What about a condom?"

"I want to taste you. Don't worry. I know every lover you've ever had."

He wrapped his hand around Ryan's cock before he sucked it into his mouth. Ryan thrust, trying to get deeper in, but Jason pinned him down with one hand on his hip. Taking control, he proved just how experienced he was. He swallowed until the head of Ryan's penis hit the back of his throat. Jason worked Ryan's cock with his hand and mouth, giving no respite or time to think about anything. He wanted Ryan totally wrapped up in the moment, not worrying about the future.

"Jason, I'm gonna…" Ryan warned, but Jason didn't pull away.

Everything. That's what he wanted from Ryan, not just the man's cum, but the man's heart as well. Jason swallowed Ryan down again and the other man came, flooding Jason's throat and mouth. Jason eased off enough to ensure he didn't gag, but he drank down every drop spilling from Ryan.

While Ryan shuddered through his climax, Jason wet his fingers and rubbed them over Ryan's hole. Ryan grabbed his legs behind the knees, pulling them up and out, offering Jason more access. Jason licked Ryan's cock clean and sucked gently while he slowly eased his fingers into Ryan's ass.

Jason let Ryan's softened cock slide from his mouth as he continued to stretch his lover, wanting to just bury himself as deep as he could into Ryan, but not wanting to hurt him either.

"Please, I need more," Ryan pleaded as he rocked on Jason's fingers.

Glancing down, Jason noticed Ryan's dick was making a valiant effort to harden again. He rolled to the side of the bed, reaching for the lube and condoms in the night stand drawer. Crowing in delight, he held them up. Jason struggled to get the condom on, the lube coated over his cock and some in Ryan to ease his way.

After what felt like an hour, but was probably only a minute or two, Jason knelt between Ryan's thighs and positioned the head of his prick at Ryan's opening. As he sank into the moist heat, he stared into Ryan's eyes, hoping his lover could see all the love Jason felt for him shining in his own gaze.

They gasped as Jason buried himself balls deep and stopped for a second. Ryan sighed and clenched his inner muscles, telling Jason it was okay to move. Jason gripped Ryan's hips and began to thrust in and out, driving cries from Ryan with each entry. Ryan braced his hands against the headboard, pushing back against Jason.

Their rhythm picked up speed until the bed banged against the wall and grunts filled the air. Pleasure tingled along Jason's spine, pooling at the base. His balls drew tight to his body as his climax began to rocket through him. He peeled one hand away from Ryan's hip to fist the man's cock. He could tell they were both poised on the edge and just one more push would tilt them over.

"Come again, Ryan. I want to feel you come on my cock."

His harsh order was just what Ryan needed. His climax didn't have quite the same force as the first one, but the massaging contractions of Ryan's ass around Jason's cock were more than enough to get Jason off.

Jason filled the condom with a shout. He jerked and trembled as waves of pleasure rippled through him until all strength drained from his muscles. His brain worked just enough to remind him to roll to the side before collapsing to the bed. Lying on his back, he stared up at the ceiling, chest heaving.

"Wow."

Ryan's breathless single-word verdict brought a smile to Jason's lips. He rested his clean hand on Ryan's chest, feeling the man's racing heart under his palm. When his own pulse slowed, he climbed from the bed and wandered to the bathroom, where he disposed of the condom before cleaning up. He wetted a washcloth and brought it back to take care of Ryan.

He tossed the cloth back towards the bathroom before shifting Ryan around to get them both under the covers. Jason settled down, embracing Ryan from behind, pressing his chest tight to Ryan's back. He brushed a kiss over the nape of Ryan's neck.

"Do you think you can sleep now?"

"I'll admit your sleep inducing methods are quite impressive." Ryan entwined their fingers. "Thank you, Jason."

"For what?"

Ryan shrugged. "For loving me. For believing in me. For a thousand different things you do for me that I can't begin to tell you about."

"You do the same things for me. You can ask Roland because I've never even considered giving something up for any man. You're the only guy I'd walk away from the project for, especially if it was the best way to keep you safe." Jason buried his face in Ryan's sweat-drenched curls. "I love you, Ryan Christopher, and no matter what happens tomorrow, I always will."

Ryan brought their joined hands up to his mouth and pressed a kiss to the back of Jason's. Silence fell between them and Jason listened as Ryan's breathing deepened. When he was certain Ryan was asleep, Jason untangled himself and climbed out of bed. He padded over to the window and stared out at the looming facade of the monastery.

Maybe it was a figment of his imagination, but darkness shrouded the building and a veil of evil hung over it. He didn't want Ryan to go back in there, but he understood why Ryan felt he had to go. Jason planned on being with his boyfriend every step of the way to protect him the best he could.

"You better not hurt him," he warned the spirits in St. Xavier. "If one hair on his head gets harmed, I will raze the building to the ground and you'll never get a chance at revenge. I know that's what you want. You're not looking for forgiveness. You've had too long to build up your anger. You're looking to exact revenge on the bastard who destroyed your lives."

Jason glanced back over his shoulder to where Ryan lay, asleep in his bed. When he looked back at St. Xavier, he thought he saw a flash of light in one of the fourth floor windows.

"I don't care what you do with Adler or Ellen. They deserve to pay for their crimes. Just don't hurt Ryan and I'll turn a blind eye to whatever you do."

Having made his deal with the spirits haunting the old monastery, Jason made his way back to bed and snuggled close to Ryan again. He needed to take his own advice and get some sleep. Tomorrow would test all of them, but hopefully it would bring the whole nasty issue to a close, if only for Ryan's sake.

* * * *

Conversation around the breakfast table was kept light. They all knew it was the day of reckoning for Ellen Fitzroy and Joseph Adler. Ryan couldn't even bring himself to call Joseph a bishop anymore. Not only had the man committed crimes against Sister Ann, Father Clennan and the Church, but he'd betrayed Ryan at the deepest level. Never would Ryan consider Joseph Adler his grandfather.

He looked at the phone on the table. "I don't think I can do it. He knows me too well. He'll figure out I'm lying and the whole plan will fall apart."

Jason set down his fork and reached for Ryan's hand. "Are you asking me to call him?"

Ryan nodded. "Would you?"

"Of course. I'll have to change the script a bit though." Jason reached for the phone. "Are we all ready for this?"

Ryan stood and began pacing the kitchen as Roland and Burt nodded. He longed to run away to his little spot in the garden, but knew that wouldn't help anyone. The time was now. "Do it," Ryan said, coming to a stop at Jason's side.

"Should I put him on speaker?" Jason asked.

Ryan shook his head. "He'll be able to tell." He plopped down in Jason's lap. "Just hold it out enough that I can hear what he's saying."

"Wait!" Roland stood and yanked the phone out of Jason's hand. "You're soooo not good at this deceiving part. You can't call Adler from Ryan's phone. Use yours and act like Ryan isn't around."

Everyone at the table stared at Roland. "What?" Roland rolled his eyes dramatically. "You don't think I've ever deceived someone? Wake up, people. I am who I am."

"We'll discuss this later," Burt said.

Roland blew out a breath and patted Burt's hand. "I would never deceive you, sweetums."

Jason chuckled and pulled out his own phone. "What's the number?"

Ryan rattled it off before leaning close enough to hear both sides of the conversation.

The phone rang four times before Joseph finally answered. "You've got a lot of nerve calling me after what happened."

"Well, you see, I have this problem. It's not really a problem, I guess, at least not mine," Jason began. "But my crew had to rip up the floorboards on the fourth floor, and guess what they uncovered in the corner office? That *was* Father Clennan's office, wasn't it?

There was a moment of silence before Adler spoke. "Well, are you planning to tell me, or just continue this little game of yours?"

"Oh, I assure you, I don't play games. I'm holding in my hand a letter signed by Father Clennan and witnessed by a Father Paul Burger. According to the letter, Father Joseph Adler raped and imprisoned Sister Ann Cawfield on the fourth floor of St. Xavier Monastery."

"That's a lie!" Adler bellowed.

"It goes on to say that Ellen Fitzroy from St. Nicholas' Orphanage delivered Sister Ann's child, a daughter, by the way, on June seventeenth, nineteen sixty-two. According to Father Clennan, Ellen Fitzroy left St. Xavier with the child despite protests from Sister Ann." Jason chuckled into the phone. "Now, how would I know all of this if the letter wasn't currently in my hand?"

"What do you want?"

"I don't understand why, but it seems very important to Ryan that you and Ellen Fitzroy apologise to the spirits in the monastery. If the two of you will come down here and honestly give your apologies, I'll give you the letter and all will be forgotten."

"Why should I trust you?" Adler asked.

"Because I'm a businessman, Bishop Adler. All I want is to get my project finished so gay men from all over the world can invade your little town and fuck to their hearts' content. And dwelling on what happened over fifty years ago isn't making me any money. Now, do we have a deal, or should I just drop this letter by the police station?"

After another long pause, Adler cleared his throat. "Ellen and I will meet you, and you alone, at the front entrance. I don't want to see Ryan anywhere. Do we understand each other?"

"Of course. I'll expect you within the hour." Jason hung up the phone and tossed it onto the table. "Well, that went well."

Ryan moved to straddle Jason's lap. "You do realise I'll be inside the building waiting for them, right?"

Jason lifted his hand to the back of Ryan's neck and pulled him in for a deep kiss. Ryan could taste the fear on Jason's tongue as if it were a tangible thing. Breaking the kiss, Jason pressed his cheek against Ryan's. "I love you."

"I know. And I love you. Which is why I have to follow this through to the end."

* * * *

"They'll be here any minute," Ryan told the grotesque vision of Father Clennan. "Promise me you'll accept his apology and move on."

"I promise nothing but to see the man responsible for my death pay for his crime."

Ryan shook his head. "That would make you no better than he is."

"I'm dead by his hands. Do you really think I care who the better man is?"

The last thing Ryan wanted was another blood bath. St. Xavier had seen more than its share of death. "Please. I can't allow him in here if I think you're going to kill him. After everything you've suffered, you deserve to rise not fall."

The apparition shook its head. *"I've already condemned myself to a life of hell, and nothing would please me more than to torture Joseph Adler for eternity."*

Ryan heard the front door open and knew his time was up. "Sister Ann deserves an apology. If you kill them as soon as they enter, that gift will be taken from her."

"She deserves nothing!" Father Clennan screamed before disappearing.

From his hiding place on the third floor landing, Ryan heard Jason's voice. *No.* He'd given Jason strict orders not to enter the building. Ryan closed his eyes and silently begged Father Clennan and Sister Ann to stay away from the man he loved.

"Give me the letter," Joseph blustered.

"Not until you apologise. I believe Sister Ann is trapped on the fourth floor where you kept her a prisoner for nine months. Shall we start with her, or would you like to apologise to Father Clennan first?" Jason asked.

"I will not apologise to Clennan. It was Sister Ann who murdered him."

"Liar!" Father Clennan screamed, rattling the windows.

Afraid for everyone involved, Ryan stood and held up his hands. He ignored Ellen and addressed Adler. "Please," he begged. "Please own up to what you did."

Halfway up the stairs to the third floor, Adler stopped. He narrowed his eyes at Ryan before looking behind him at Jason. "What did I tell you about seeing Ryan here?"

The moment the question left his mouth, Adler was pushed backwards by unseen hands. As if in slow motion, Ryan watched the older man fall and knock Jason off his feet. Ryan started down the steps, pushing by Ellen, but couldn't reach the man he loved in time to save him from the first smack of his head against the step.

"No!" Ryan screamed, climbing over Adler's body to reach Jason.

"Joseph," Ellen called, bending to check on Adler.

Ryan couldn't care less about the older man at that point. He knelt beside Jason's unconscious body on the second floor landing. "Jason? Come on, sweetheart, open your eyes." Ryan reached down to check Jason's pulse and was relieved to find it. Pulling out his phone, Ryan called Roland.

"What happened?" Roland answered.

"Jason fell down the steps. I need Burt to come and get him out of here before something worse happens to him."

"Is he conscious?" Roland asked.

"No, but his pulse is steady. He's on the second floor landing. I have to get Adler up to the fourth floor before Father Clennan has another go at him."

"It's not worth it, Ryan. Just get the fuck out of there."

"I can't. I have to finish this thing once and for all." Ryan ended the call and bent to give Jason a soft kiss. "I love you," he whispered.

Turning his attention to Adler, Ryan was pleased to see Ellen had the man sitting up. "Let's go," he said, motioning up the flight of stairs.

"No. I'm done," Adler spat.

"The hell you are." Ryan grabbed what little hair Adler still had on the back of his head and pulled him to his feet.

"Stop it. You're hurting him," Ellen cried.

Anger like nothing he'd ever felt seemed to take over Ryan. He backhanded Ellen across the face. "Shut the fuck up!"

Ellen's eyes rounded as she covered her abused cheek with her hand.

Ryan heard an evil laugh inside his head and realised Father Clennan's spirit had entered him. "Is this what you did to Jack Dorsel? You got into his head and drove him insane?"

"I took the problem directly to you, Deacon Christopher. I couldn't take the chance that I'd be trapped another fifty years in this hell-hole," Clennan answered. "You need me right now. You're not strong enough to do this on your own."

Ryan's body jerked as he tried to mentally extract Clennan's spirit. The moment he turned Ellen and gave her a push towards the third floor, he knew he hadn't been successful. *Please help me, God.*

"Move," he ordered Adler and Ellen. Ryan maintained the grip on Adler's hair as he marched the two of them up the steps. "You're a filthy fucker, Adler, hiding behind your pristine robe when your soul is as black as mine."

Adler swung out behind him and tried to knock Ryan's hand away. Ryan's grip increased. He shook Adler's head, causing the man to cry out in pain. "Just one more flight," Ryan said in Adler's ear as they reached the third floor landing.

Ryan yanked Adler's head down at the bottom of the steps. "You recognise that pool of blood?"

"It can't be," Adler said, his voice shaking. "That was years ago."

Ellen seemed to be in a trance of fear as she continued to climb the steps. Good. The bitch deserved to be afraid. Ryan chuckled in a voice that wasn't his own. "Keep going," he ordered, giving Adler a push up the stairs.

"She seduced me. When she got pregnant, she tried to tell everyone she'd been raped, but that's not true," Adler babbled.

Ryan opened his mouth to contradict Adler when he noticed the bloody nun at the top of the stairs. Sister Ann backed away the closer they got to the fourth floor. Once Ryan had Adler and Ellen in the same room with Sister Ann, his body began shaking.

"Release him," Ann commanded.

Ryan felt an internal tug of war and knew Sister Ann was trying to help him get Clennan's spirit out of his body.

"I'll leave Adler to you as long as I can watch and you leave my grandson out of it," Ann said.

Ryan's body collapsed onto the floor. He opened his eyes, but when he tried to sit up, he found he was once again being held in place by unseen shackles.

Adler dropped to his knees and held his hands up in prayer. "Please forgive me."

Ann stared down at Adler with contempt in her eyes. "Forgive you?" She laughed, the sound travelling up Ryan's spine like fingernails on a chalkboard. "You raped me! You imprisoned me and took my child! You deserve no forgiveness."

Sister Ann turned her back on the crying man and walked towards the window.

As Ryan and Ellen watched, Adler's body rose off the floor, much to his displeasure. "Let me go!" Adler screamed, swinging his arms and kicking his legs.

The older man levitated for several moments before being thrown across the room. Adler's body slammed against the panelled wall before coming to rest in a heap on the floor.

Father Clennan appeared out of the darkened corner and stood over Adler. "Confess your sins and prepare to die," he told the cowering man.

"She was so beautiful," Adler said between sobs. "I tried to stay away…"

"You drove her insane!" Clennan accused. "Then you condemned me to watch over your mistake all these years."

"I tried to fix it. I tried to take Maria and Ryan under my wing and protect them," Adler continued.

"You tried to ease your own guilt with more lies," Ryan said, unable to hold his tongue.

Father Clennan turned and addressed Ryan. "I no longer care what happens to this man. You were right. He's not worth it. What would you have me do with him?"

Ryan shook his head. Being in the position to decide someone's fate wasn't something he was comfortable with, especially when that someone was a rapist and murderer. However, Ryan knew if he declined to make the decision, Father Clennan would kill Adler without a second thought. "Bring the Archbishop here and let him confess his crimes. Moreover, call the police and see that he pays for them."

"No," Adler shook his head. "I won't do it."

Ryan stared at Adler. "It's the only choice you have if you want to walk out of here alive."

"Then I'd rather die." Although obviously still shaken, Adler pushed to his feet and strode towards the window. As if on automatic pilot, Adler unlocked and opened the window before looking back at Ryan. "I really did try to do right by you."

Ryan snorted. "Perhaps you should have loved and supported me, then, instead of condemning me for being me."

With a slow shake of his head, Adler threw himself out the window. Ryan gasped when he heard the thunk as Adler's body hit the cement driveway below. He swallowed the bile that threatened to rise up and out. "Are you satisfied?" he asked Father Clennan.

Still staring out of the window, Father Clennan shook his head. "No. Why is that?"

The answer finally struck Ryan. "Because you still haven't forgiven yourself for what happened so long ago." Ryan was released from his shackles and got to his feet. He felt the burn of tears as he tried to remember the events he'd been shown. "Despite what you feel, that you did wrong, I know that you tried to make it right before you died. Now you have to realise there was nothing else you could have done to prevent what happened that day."

Father Clennan's watery gaze travelled to Sister Ann. "I'm sorry I didn't believe you."

Ann nodded as Father Clennan's spirit vanished in the glow of bright light.

Ryan gestured to Ellen, who had taken refuge in the corner of the room. "What about her? Will you show her the same mercy you showed Father Clennan?"

Sister Ann refused to look at Ellen. "She did me a favour when she killed me. I wasn't right. I'd lost too much by then."

"She's old," Ryan reminded Sister Ann. "Let her live out the few years she has left knowing Adler lied to her about the affair." Ryan stared at Ellen. "You loved him, didn't you?"

"He told me if I took the child he would leave the priesthood and we could become a family," Ellen admitted.

"So why did you stay with him all these years?" Ryan asked.

"He watched me murder a woman, and I'm ashamed to admit it, but I still loved him."

Ryan returned his attention to Sister Ann. "Let her go. Please. Maybe in showing mercy to someone who doesn't deserve it, you'll be able to move on."

Ann waved her hand. "Go," she ordered Ellen.

Before Ellen had a chance to make it out of the room, Ryan stopped her. "If the police have questions about Adler's death, you will verify that you saw him jump from the window. I won't have Jason under suspicion for anything that's happened here today."

Ellen gave a shaky nod and ran out of the room.

Left alone with Sister Ann, Ryan knew it was his one and probably only chance to speak to his grandmother. "Do you know what happened to my mother?"

Ann shook her head. "She was lost to me the day they took her from my arms. My whole world has become this suite of rooms. I know nothing beyond these walls."

Ryan nodded. It wasn't the answer he'd hoped for, but at least he knew the spirits of St. Xavier weren't responsible for his mom's abandonment. "Will you be able to move on now?"

Ann shook her head once more. "I don't want to go."

"What do you mean? I thought the whole purpose of this was to help you move on?" Why had he risked his life?

"I'd much rather stay and watch over my grandson."

Ryan studied the room. "I'd have to discuss that with Jason. You know he's turning this place into a hotel, right? I don't think he'd appreciate you haunting his guests." The fallen expression on Ann's face nearly broke Ryan's heart. "Don't worry. We'll figure something out."

Epilogue

One Year Later

Ryan shut down his computer and stood to stretch out the kinks in his back. Although it didn't happen often, Jason had been called out of town the previous morning to deal with a mini-crisis at one of the resorts. Ryan had discovered early on in their relationship that he couldn't sleep without Jason pressed against his back. He usually travelled with his partner, but *Xavier Resort* had a large party scheduled to arrive the previous evening, and Ryan had been needed to welcome them.

It was still hard for Ryan to believe how much he loved living and working at the resort. He continually surprised himself with how comfortable he'd become openly discussing the sexual playrooms and hidden areas of the garden with the guests. Perhaps it had to do with the accepting atmosphere created by both staff and guests.

Ryan locked the door to the office he shared with Jason and stuck his head into Roland's office across the hall. "Any news on the permits for the new headquarters?"

Roland glanced up from his monitor. "Hank said he should have them in hand by the end of the week. We should be able to break ground Monday."

"Excellent." Ryan couldn't be happier that Jason had decided to move his headquarters a little closer to home. In a year's time, they'd all have brand new offices in a six-story building at the edge of town.

Roland had been the catalyst for the move. After Burt had had a dangerous run-in with a thug on the streets of Los Angeles that resulted in a gunshot wound to the shoulder, Roland had begged Jason to get them both out of California. Burt was currently working for the local police department and, according to Roland, happier than he'd ever been.

"I'm going down to the garden. If Jason gets back before I do, can you point him my way?" he asked.

Roland glanced at the clock. "As long as he gets here in the next ten minutes. After that I'm outta here. Burt's agreed to meet me for a pedicure in town."

Ryan couldn't help but chuckle. The thought of the big policeman having his toenails painted was too much. "I'd like to see that, but why don't you just have it done downstairs in the spa?"

Roland shook a pen in Ryan's direction. "He refused to have it done here because he doesn't want anyone to know. Tease him and I'll tell Jason you told me about the two of you getting that body wax done last time you were in San Francisco."

Ryan held up his hands in surrender. He couldn't begin to compete with Roland when it came to blackmail games. "My lips are sealed."

Leaving the small suite of offices at the back of the first floor, Ryan wandered out to the garden. He waved to a small group of men lounging beside the newly installed swimming pool. There were no dress codes at *Xavier Resort* and many of the guests preferred to either walk around nude or just in a robe of some kind. Surprisingly, it hadn't taken Ryan long at all to get accustomed to the lack of modesty. Although he still preferred to wear clothes while working, he'd learned to enjoy swimming in the nude.

Continuing along the path, Ryan spotted his grandmother peeking into one of the private gardens. He shook his head and walked up behind her. "Haven't we talked about this? No spying on the guests."

It hadn't taken much convincing on Ryan's part to get Jason to agree to let his grandmother stick around. Jason's only stipulation was that she move out of the building and promise not to invade anyone's privacy, especially Ryan and Jason's. Ann had quickly agreed and had since spent her days walking around the grounds, helping the gardeners tend to the flowers with unseen care.

Ryan didn't understand it, but for some reason he was now the only one who could see Ann. Even Jason, who had seen Ann's ghost on several occasions, no longer could.

Ann turned around, flustered at getting caught. *"I still can't get used to seeing men do those things to each other."*

Ryan gestured for Ann to follow him and led the way to their special place. The garden he thought of as his sanctuary now was home to a large statue of Sister Ann holding an infant. Of course no one but their immediate group knew the significance of the statue, but it seemed to please Ann to be near it.

Ryan took up his usual spot on the grass and pillowed his hands behind his head. Jason had offered to put a bench or a table and chairs in the garden, but Ryan liked his bed of grass. "If I fall asleep, wake me up. Jason should be home any time and he'd never find me out here."

"Who're you talking to?" Jason asked, stepping into view.

Ryan shielded the sun with his hand and smiled up at his gorgeous lover. "My nosy grandma. Did you just get back?" He held out his arms and welcomed the press of Jason's body on top of him.

Jason gazed down at his lover. "Yep. I didn't even bother going inside. Just called Roland from the car as I drove in and he said you'd be out here. "

He gave Ryan a long lingering kiss, savouring his unique flavour. A soft laugh drifted in through the hedges surrounding Ryan's quiet place. Jason pulled away and sat, nudging Ryan to get him to sit up as well.

"I missed you," Ryan seemed disappointed Jason hadn't taken the kiss further.

"I missed you too, and I'm not opposed to fucking you right out in the open, but I have something I wanted to give you." He fumbled in his pocket, inexplicably nervous all of a sudden.

"Really?" Ryan almost clapped his hands, excited like a kid at Christmas.

"Yes. Didn't you get presents when you were a kid?" Jason got the box out of his pocket before glancing up at Ryan.

The younger man stared up at Sister Ann's statue with a sad expression on his face. "No, I didn't get presents. My step-father spent all his cash on alcohol. My foster mom didn't have money for anything extra. Besides, I was taught not to want material things."

"Oh, honey, I'm sorry." Jason vowed to shower Ryan with gifts, inexpensive or as costly as he could find. He would make up for all the things Ryan had missed as a kid.

Ryan looked at him with a slight smile. "I'm not complaining. In the end, I got the best present in the world. You."

Jason couldn't let that statement pass without rewarding his boyfriend. He leant in and kissed Ryan again. He swept his tongue into Ryan's mouth, teasing and stroking, until Ryan grasped his shoulders, relaxing into him. Jason eased back while Ryan whimpered in protest.

"After I give you this, I'm going to carry you home and make love to you all evening and the rest of the night. But you have to let me get this out."

He picked up the box from where he'd dropped it. He held it out to Ryan. "I found this up in the corner office on the fourth floor. I thought you might like it."

Ryan turned the box around in his hands and Jason had never been so scared, not even when opening a new resort. He hoped Ryan would like it. Ryan opened the box and gasped as the dying sunlight glinted off the bright gold band.

He watched as Ryan tugged the ring out and held it up. "Always and forever," he read. "Ahhh, that's so sweet."

"Read the inside," Jason prompted.

Ryan smiled as he did as instructed. "Even After Death."

Ryan's expression melted Jason's heart. Jason shrugged in response. "It seemed fitting in a way."

Ryan's head tilted in the way Jason had come to recognise as his listening to Ann pose. Tears welled in his lover's green eyes and Jason wrapped Ryan in a tight embrace.

"What is it, love?"

"My grandmother says this is her ring, and she's so happy I have it."

Jason pressed a kiss to Ryan's cheek as he slipped the ring onto Ryan's finger. "Maybe someday we can go and get married legally somewhere, but for now, this is my pledge to you. I'll love you always and forever, even after death. I can't see my life without you anymore, and I hope I never have to find out what it's like."

"I promise the same thing. I never thought I'd ever be truly happy, but from the moment I met you, I discovered I deserved to be happy and have a great life with someone who loved me. I love you, Jason Bentley. Now take me home and fuck me silly."

"Gladly, love."

Jason pushed to his feet and swept Ryan into his arms. As they left Ryan's sanctuary, a gentle breeze brushed over Jason's cheek and he swore he heard Sister Anne whisper, *"Thank you."*

"You're welcome." He smiled softly as he carried Ryan to their cottage; a home filled with the spirit of love and happiness banishing the haunted past of St. Xavier.

About the Authors

Carol Lynne

An avid reader for years, one day Carol Lynne decided to write her own brand of erotic romance. Carol juggles between being a full-time mother and a full-time writer. These days, you can usually find Carol either cleaning jelly out of the carpet or nestled in her favourite chair writing steamy love scenes.

T.A. Chase

There is beauty in every kind of love, so why not live a life without boundaries? Experiencing everything the world offers fascinates TA and writing about the things that make each of us unique is how TA shares those insights. TA lives in the Midwest with a wonderful partner of twelve years. When not writing, TA's watching movies, reading and living life to the fullest.

Both Carol and T.A. love to hear from readers.

You can find their contact information, website details and author profile pages at http://www.total-e-bound.com.

Total-E-Bound Publishing

www.total-e-bound.com

Take a look at our exciting range of literagasmic™
erotic romance titles and discover pure quality
at Total-E-Bound.

9493284R0

Made in the USA
Lexington, KY
02 May 2011